The Not So Perfect Storm

The Not So Perfect Storm

DOG AGILITY TALES

Ron Etherton

IMAGO
P R E S S
TUCSON ARIZONA

Published in the United States of America by:

Imago Press
3710 East Edison
Tucson AZ 85716

Names, characters, places, and incidents, unless otherwise specifically noted, are either the product of the author's imagination or are used fictitiously.

Library of Congress Catalogue Number: 2012943511

Book and Cover Design by Leila Joiner
Cover illustration: Green Water Twist © romarti

Photo Credits:
   Page 6: Clark Kranz
   Page 28: Tien tran Photography
   Pg 222: Clark Kranz
   Pg 262: Pet Personalities - Allisa
   Back cover photo: Bill Newcomb Photography

   All other photos, including front cover photo:
   courtesy of Ron Etherton or friends

ISBN 978-1-935437-66-6
ISBN 1-935437-66-6

Printed in the United States of America on Acid-Free Paper

To my best friend, Anne,
my wife for 48 years

Preface

Once upon a time in a land not so far away, people wanted to have fun with their dogs. Some had handsome conformation animals, but jogging around the show ring really wasn't enough exercise. Others participated in obedience trials. Teaching a dog to sit, stay, and come was important, but had limited entertainment value. Athletic field dogs possessed marvelous talents for retrieving game, but many owners were not keen to hunt.

In the late 1980's, the sport of dog agility came to the United States from England. Enthusiasts assembled bulky homemade obstacles using PVC pipe and wood. Enterprising businesses began producing equipment. Tools of the trade were expensive, so small groups formed clubs and pooled their resources to make ends meet. These pioneers encouraged each other, traded training tips, and proudly presented exhibitions to the public.

In the early 1990's, agility clubs held trials around the country. Gas was cheap, so people and their dogs traveled freely between Washington, Oregon, California, and Arizona. Other centers of activity ranged from New England to Texas.

Almost all dogs were capable of learning agility skills: pugs, poodles, retrievers, shepherds, terriers, Newfoundlands, and mixed breeds. The sport evolved quickly. Soon it became apparent that certain breeds learned quicker, ran faster, and were more athletic. Herding breeds, such as Shetland sheepdogs, Australian shepherds, and border collies, began to dominate the sport.

Over the next decade, the sport grew out of its youthful innocence and expanded to include world competitions and television specials, providing business opportunities for trainers, marketers, specialty magazines, and equipment manufacturers.

You are about to read a fictional account of the people and their dogs involved in the sport during those early years. The heroes in this story are the magnificent canines: our contestants and, more importantly, our companions.

1 The Hurricane

On August 14, 1992, a tropical wave of low pressure moved off the west coast of Africa. Under the influence of a ridge of high pressure to the north, the wave tracked quickly westward. Thunderstorm activity grew more concentrated, and narrow spiral rain-bands developed around a center of circulation. The tropical depression earned an infamous honor as the first Atlantic storm named that year. An eye formed, and Andrew attained hurricane status on August 22.

A day later, Andrew was a category five monster. It slammed into southern Florida with peak winds of 175 MPH that blew away the instruments used to measure them. Twenty-five minutes after landfall, Andrew bulls-eyed near Homestead in Dade County. The worst damage occurred not from straight-line winds, but from vortices, or "mini-whirls" that behaved like embedded tornadoes.

Survivors wondered if this had been their Armageddon. After ravaging southern Florida, Andrew raced across the Gulf of Mexico, took a capricious turn to the North, and roared through southeastern Louisiana, dumping a foot of rain.

Desperate mothers were reported to be collecting water in baby bottles from mud puddles. Residents sat in the wreckage of their homes, holding shotguns to ward off looters. Police warned of violence unless food and shelter arrived quickly. Three days later, Dade County Emergency Management Director, Kate Hale, lamented during a nationally televised news conference, "Where in the hell is the cavalry on this one? They keep saying we're getting supplies. For God's sake, where are they?"

President Bush promised, "Help is on the way." But help was several days away. FEMA fiddled while the survivors burned with anger. A massive waste of relief supplies, fractured transportation, and petty jurisdictional rifts left the victims wondering if they were living in a third world country.

Hurricane Andrew became the most expensive natural disaster in U.S. history. The price tag in Dade County alone would eventually climb to $25 billion. The name Andrew was retired and will never be used again for an Atlantic hurricane. The toll in human suffering was matched only by the cruel fate of abandoned pets and livestock. From all over the United States, volunteers arrived to help fill the bureaucratic vacuum.

The dog pulled hard on the chain that anchored him to a shed while his master loaded the truck. He wanted to jump onto the rear flatbed again and feel the wind in his face, filling his nose with wonderful smells. He wanted to retrieve the birds that fell from the sky after the thunder stick boomed.

He resumed digging a shallow trench in the semi-circle drawn by the chain pulled to its limit, but stopped when he saw the truck drive away. The wind blew harder and rain began to pelt him, so the dog withdrew to the protection of the shed. The sky noise grew louder and more frequent, but the master had trained him to ignore loud noises like the thunder stick.

Soon, the trench he had dug in front of the shed filled with water. The dog had never felt wind so strong, not even when he rode in the truck. The shed shook violently and burst apart around him. Boards flew skyward and the wind carried them away. He realized he was free and ran to the road.

The chain, still attached to a small section of the shed, bounced along the gravel road behind him. The dog ran at full speed for a few minutes, and then all the familiar scents disappeared. He shook to displace water from his wavy coat and trotted back home. The shed was gone, and the fields were flooded. Hungry, he trotted to the master's door and scratched in vain. He curled up on the front stoop, wet, hungry, and alone.

The storm abated overnight. The next morning he scratched again on the front door, but no one came. The truck had not returned. Reluctantly, he trotted to the road, dragging the chain and its burden, to search for food.

2   The Rescue

Noah and Judy Webster took a week off from teaching school in Jacksonville, arrived at the Dade County Animal Rescue Center on Monday, August 31, and volunteered to be collectors. Six exhausted helpers staffed the facility. The newcomers were told, "A bus is coming later this week. Most of these animals are going to be moved to shelters as far away as California."

The Websters were appalled to find 350 pets crowded into a barn, with the overflow dogs chained outside to fence posts, panting away in the hot sun. Some had tarp shelters, but many did not. The strong smell of urine and excrement was inescapable. One man found his dog there, but couldn't leave because the hurricane had completely destroyed his home, so he stayed in the barn.

Early the next morning, the Websters drove their van south on the Dixie highway into a landscape that might as well have been the result of a nuclear blast. Virtually every building was leveled. The storm surge from Biscayne Bay had swept aside anything passed over by Andrew. Here and there, isolated houses emerged from the flooded landscape like islands in a steamy surreal sea. A short drive to the west, alligators roamed city streets.

They parked next to a lake, or what may have been just another flooded meadow. At eight o'clock that morning the temperature was already in the low nineties, and the humidity was at least that high. The stench of gasoline, natural gas, and decaying plants and animals hung in the air like a suffocating blanket.

Judy spotted him first: a large black dog swimming across the water toward them. "Looks like some kind of retriever. Coming right at us. He could've taken the long way around on the shore, but took the shortest path. My God, I pray there aren't any gators in the water. Be careful, Noah."

Noah waded into the waist deep water. He strained to see what the dog was dragging behind him. "Here, boy. Come on." The dog swam harder and his shoulders rose high above the surface.

Noah grabbed the collar and helped the exhausted animal out of the water. Judy unclipped a six-foot chain. A bolt attached to a broken piece of wood dangled at the far end.

"It's a wonder he's still alive," Noah said. "All skin and bones. Probably hasn't eaten in days. How old would you say he is?"

Judy gently slid the dog's lips apart. "His teeth are perfectly white and very sharp. I'd guess he's less than a year old." She stroked his wet, black, wavy hair, looking for injuries, and then massaged his feet. "His toes are webbed. This is a water dog, a bird dog. My guess is we've got a flat-coated retriever."

"Does he have tags?"

"Yes, we should be able to find the owner."

Later that day, the Websters returned triumphantly to the shelter with their rescue. After several attempts, they contacted the owner on Wednesday, who decided he didn't want the retriever. "The worst hunting dog I ever owned," he complained. "I assumed the alligators got him."

A week later, the flat-coat and thirty-five other dogs were crated aboard a 727 headed to San Francisco. After they landed, the canine orphans were driven to a shelter in Santa Rosa. Local television stations sent mobile crews to cover the arrival. Spectators cheered. Some wept. Public interest seemed strong, and shelter workers hoped that all the Florida dogs would soon be adopted.

3   Park Chaos

Ben Kowalski plodded toward a bench in Sebastopol's Ives Park. California weather permitting, he came to the park every fall morning that fateful year of 1992. The old man's trousers, held in place by a pair of plaid suspenders, hung loosely on his thinning hips. His leathery skin, once tanned by years spent working outdoors, was now pale. An occasional black strand in his ashen hair escaped the unrelenting passage of time.

Ben winced in pain, instinctively grabbing his hip. He eased himself onto a bench and gazed at the bucolic setting. Ducks and geese floated effortlessly in the nearby pond. The apple tree leaves held their green longer than the nearby black oaks and big leaf maples, but had finally relented, and were the last to fall. An occasional breeze sent a shower of yellow-brown leaves cascading to the ground. He felt chilled and buttoned his sweater.

As the retired president of his own construction company, he'd accumulated a sizable retirement portfolio. In the late 1980's he'd spent mornings in Santa Rosa, watching the stock market ticker tape in his broker's office. He stopped going after his Lincoln Savings and Loans bonds collapsed to nothing. What could have been safer than investing in banks with home loans?

The memory got Ben's heart racing. Banker Charles Keating had skimmed profits and defrauded customers. The Judge gave Keating the maximum ten-year prison sentence, quoting Woody Guthrie's line: "More people have suffered from the point of a fountain pen than from a gun."

Ben recognized the lady making her way toward him. He'd seen her often at the nearby Senior Center. She had neatly coiffured silver-gray hair and wore a navy blue pants suit. Younger than he was, she always seemed to be high-spirited, perhaps too much so for Ben.

"What's on the schedule today, Doris?" Ben asked, trying to sound interested. His mind drifted as Doris explained the day's activities: arts and crafts, bingo, and aerobics. "We'd like to see you more often. You know, I'm on the volunteer committee. How would you feel about helping out at the animal shelter in Santa Rosa?"

Ben massaged his unshaven chin. "I don't know anything about animals."

"I think they just want you to walk a dog now and then."

Ben knew Doris meant well. He struggled to be polite. "Dogs are so honest. You always know where you stand with them."

"There you go. You do know about dogs. We have a group going to the shelter this afternoon. Can we count on you?"

"I'll think some on it."

Doris smiled. "We're having a dance class Friday noon at the senior center."

"I haven't danced since I lost Rebecca."

"She was a schoolteacher, wasn't she?"

"Forty years in Petaluma. After she retired, she was busier than ever...until she got sick."

Ben grew pensive. She had never complained that last awful month. Instead, she kept asking how he was holding up, giving him suggestions for coping. The day cancer won he held her hand, relieved her suffering was over.

"So many people came to the funeral," Doris said.

"I've lost touch..." Ben's voice drifted off.

Ben recalled the girl he'd loved and lost in high school, whose heart he captured before shipping out to war. It didn't matter that they never had children. They had each other, and that was enough.

"Take care, Ben," Doris said. "I hope we'll see you again soon."

After Doris left, Ben reached into his pocket and pulled out a package of peanuts. He tore open the cellophane wrap with his teeth and shook several shelled nuts into his hand. On cue, a black squirrel descended from a nearby oak tree, darted to a peanut Ben tossed from the bench, and proceeded to savor the delicacy.

"Good morning, Blackie."

Two of Blackie's friends raced down from nearby trees and chattered noisily. Ben, about to toss another peanut, saw all three beggars race for the nearest tree and scramble to safety. A large black dog raced past the bench, followed by a runner carrying a leash.

The man appeared to be about forty years old. He slowed his pace and glanced at Ben. "Good morning."

Ben glared at the intruder. "Put a leash on that dog! He's a menace, and you're a nitwit. Can't you read the park signs?"

"Sorry. Storm, come." The dog turned and raced to the man, who promptly attached the leash. "I got this dog at the shelter. I need to enroll him in an obedience class. Won't happen again, I promise."

Ben took a deep breath. Trying to act less contentious, he asked, "Is that a Labrador retriever?"

"The lady at the shelter called him a flat-coated retriever. He survived Hurricane Andrew."

"Nice looking dog. Sorry I yelled at you."

"That's okay. I deserved it. Well, we're off again." The man resumed his run, struggling to maintain control as the dog pulled him along. "Easy," he yelled. The dog pulled harder.

"What an idiot," Ben murmured to himself. Using his cane, he pushed off from the bench and trudged toward the senior center.

4 Room 55

The Sonoma County Animal Shelter needed to make hard choices. The kennels were overflowing. Dogs that couldn't find a home would end up in Room 55.

Margaret, a thirty-year-old Vet Tech, walked slowly along the row of kennels on her way to the main building. She wore glasses and kept her hair neatly cut at shoulder length. She loved animals, but the pressures of her job sometimes got her down.

The odor of unclean kennels drifted across the courtyard. Twenty hurricane dogs remained unadopted, along with many other new arrivals. The dogs lay bewildered, or paced anxiously in their kennels, often barking at nothing in particular. A placid-looking pit bull caught her eye. He followed her movements with a cold stare. Nearby, two puppies that looked like lab mixes wrestled each other. Surely, those adorable pups would be placed soon. She recognized the next dog, crouched at the back of the kennel, as a border collie, probably a female. She had an hourglass white marking on her face, and her ears were half bent. Four snow-white legs, mane, and chest contrasted with a jet-black body. She stared intently at Margaret with unblinking chestnut brown eyes.

Margaret peered into the dog's black pupils. The casual observer might have interpreted this as a stare down, but neither seemed threatened. Ten thousand years ago, hungry wolves cowered on the fringe of an ancient campfire, begging a few scraps of meat from a prehistoric band of migratory humans. Thus began the enduring symbiotic relationship between humans and canines. Margaret knelt down and softly greeted the new arrival.

"Hello, sweetheart."

The dog rose and walked cautiously forward. Margaret smiled, and the snow-white tip of the dog's full tail wagged ever so slowly. She guessed the dog's age at less than a year. She put her fingers lightly on the wire at the front of the kennel. "Aren't you pretty?"

The dog lowered her head and shifted her weight backwards. Margaret had seen this behavior before. The dog appeared hand shy and may have been abused. She hoped this pretty little female would find a home, but worried about the shyness.

Margaret walked on, and then stopped to glance back at the border collie as it stared after her.

The kennel smells were replaced by the odor of strong disinfectant as she entered the main building. She spotted the night animal control officer.

"Good morning, Derek. Beautiful morning, isn't it?"

"Gotta be better than last night." Derek folded his arms over his ill-fitting khaki uniform. The top button of his pants remained permanently unbuttoned to accommodate his potbelly. "First, I get this call about a doe that's been hit by a car in Tilden Park. Poor animal is barely alive when I get there. It has at least two broken legs, and there's blood everywhere. I tell you, it wasn't a pretty picture. I had to put it down and lift the bloody body into the truck."

"How awful."

Judy, the Chief Veterinarian, marched into the waiting room and joined Margaret and Derek. Her take-charge demeanor reminded some of a drill sergeant, but her infectious hearty laugh and keen sense of humor helped them all get through the arduous work at the shelter.

Derek continued his description of the previous night's unfortunate events. "Then we get a call from Santa Rosa about this pit bull that's running around loose. It attacks a poodle and a senior citizen out for a potty break."

"The senior or the poodle?" deadpanned Judy.

Derek looked puzzled. "What?"

Judy smiled and turned her head. "Oh, nothing."

"Are they okay?" Margaret asked.

Derek hitched up his pants. "Poodle's in emergency care."

"Any tags on the pit bull?" Judy said.

"As you can probably guess, the dog wasn't licensed. We'll hold him for the required period of time, and if we can't find the owner, I'm afraid the pit will end up in Room 55."

Judy was already several steps down the hallway and called back, "Gotta go, catch you later."

Margaret shuddered. If the dog was vicious and the owner couldn't be found, it would be euthanized. The shelter had an active adoption program, but would not allow dangerous animals to be adopted. "What about the border collie?" she asked.

"Someone dropped her off last night with no paperwork. I went to pull her out of the kennel this morning, but she was having no part of it. I finally had to put on the lion gloves and use a noose to pull her out. She spent the whole time trying to bite me, thrashing around like a wounded animal. Judy examined her and almost got nailed. I tried to help hold her down, but she rolled on her back and was absolutely frantic. That dog is not adoptable."

"She seems so sweet, I can't believe it. There's a border collie rescue group in Santa Rosa. They find homes for dogs who train for dog sports like fly ball or agility."

"Agility? What's that?"

"It's like the steeplechase jumping that horses do, jumping over hurdles and things like that. I think the man who adopted the flat-coated retriever a few weeks ago, one of the hurricane dogs, had that in mind."

"Yeah, I remember that black dog. Looked like it had field trial potential. Well, see ya." Derek hiked up his pants and left for home.

Over the next several days Margaret made short stops to speak to the border collie. Before leaving work one afternoon, she knelt and put her fingers on the kennel door. "Well, hello. How was your day?"

The dog came bounding over. Her tail wagged so vigorously, her entire rear end moved. She cocked her head to the right. She had such an intense, intelligent look. Being confined in a kennel all day is hard on any dog, much less a high-spirited dog like this one, Margaret thought.

She was surprised by a voice behind her. "The ID tag on the kennel says her name is Myst."

Margaret turned around, surprised to see an old man standing nearby. "That's short for Mystery," she said. "Someone dropped her off one night without leaving any name or background information."

"Is she a sheepdog?" the man asked.

"Could be. She's a border collie...like in the movie, 'Babe.' They're very intelligent."

"I don't see movies much anymore. I'm Ben. I've been helping out the last few days, taking her for walks. Will she be adopted soon?"

"I hope so. The problem is most people want a dog like one they've seen in a movie. Later, they decide the breed is not for them."

"Is that bad?"

"Every time Walt Disney releases '101 Dalmatians,' you can be sure the shelters will be receiving Dalmatians several months later. Many families haven't done their homework when selecting a border collie. If left alone, almost all will get into trouble. They dig, chew, bark, and do the things that 'bad dogs' do. Of course, they aren't really bad, they're just bored."

"Maybe Myst would be a good dog for me."

Margaret didn't want to hurt the old man's feelings, but suspected the border collie would be much too active for him. "Do you have a big yard?"

"Sure, big yard, fenced."

"Well, she'd need lots of exercise. Border collies are very loyal and affectionate. She'd be a wonderful pet for the right owner."

After a pause, Ben said, "I think she has something wrong with her foot. I noticed a limp when I walked her on the pavement. Maybe a front leg."

"Really? Let's check it out."

Margaret clapped her hands lightly, and the dog came bounding over to the door of the kennel and cautiously placed her left front foot on the wire door. Margaret gently rubbed her paw. Suddenly, the dog yelped and pulled away.

"I'm sorry. What's the problem?" She opened the kennel door. "Good girl." She extended her hand and let it go limp and motionless. The dog sniffed her hand and touched a finger with the tip of her tongue. Cautiously, Margaret examined the paw. She stroked the top, and then the bottom, touching the pads. The dog acted antsy. "What's the problem?" she said again in a soothing voice. She examined a nail. Moving to the next nail, she felt sharp splinters. The nail was shattered. Myst yelped and snapped at Margaret's hand.

"You poor baby." She turned to Ben. "That must really hurt! I'll have a vet check it out tomorrow."

Margaret hurried to the parking lot. Fog was accumulating on the western hills, and a cold afternoon breeze cut through her green lab coat.

The next morning a new group of dogs had arrived. The pit bull was gone, and so were the lab mix pups. The pups had surely been adopted, but the pit bull had probably been put down. The border collie's kennel was empty as well. She greeted the volunteer working the desk. "What's on the agenda today?"

"Judy wants you to help in room 55. She's getting things ready."

Margaret's voice dropped. "Oh. The pit bull?"

"I'm not sure."

Margaret felt light-headed as she put on her lab coat. Her arms felt weak. She stopped at the supply cabinet and pulled out a zippered plastic bag. Her shallow breaths made her more aware of her pounding heart. She entered Room 55 and nodded at Judy.

Judy pressed the play button on her tape recorder and adjusted her earphones. She had a collection of books on tape. It may have helped take her mind off the grim task. She prepared a syringe of sodium pentobarbital. It would be fast and painless.

A tranquilized dog lay on the table behind Judy. Its blue tongue hung limply out the left side of its mouth. A pair of chestnut brown eyes gazed vacantly at a wall. Margaret approached the table, and gasped. "Oh, my God."

Her heart was pounding, her hands cold. It wasn't the pit bull. It was Myst. "There's a mistake," she stammered, her voice trailing off.

"Are you sure? Let me check again." Judy studied the clipboard attached to the table. "Border collie. Aggressive. Not adoptable. Holding time expired." She paused, then asked, "Are you okay? Do you want me to get someone else to help today?"

"I know this dog." Tears welled in Margaret's eyes. "I think she needs another chance." The tears flowed freely down her cheeks. "I know someone who will adopt her."

"Are you sure?" Judy put her hand lightly on Margaret's arm. "I guess we can keep her another few days. Stay with her while she comes out of the anesthetic. I'll be helping in the spay neuter clinic the rest of the morning."

Margaret sat on a stool next to Myst. Her body shook as she sobbed. After several minutes, she took a few deep breaths and started trimming the dog's nails.

5   BI-TO

Liam Gallagher taught science at Sonoma Central High. His marriage was in shambles. His wife had left him. He went through the motions, acting as though nothing had happened, but he felt like a forty-year-old failure.

He never saw it coming until he discovered his wife's secret e-mail account. Looking back, he should have seen the clues. Myra, a real estate agent, spent long weekends hosting open houses and made frequent trips to Reno for conventions. Sometimes, when he answered the phone, he got only a dial tone. At least they had no children, and because Myra's income far exceeded his teacher's salary, there would be no alimony. After she moved out, he existed in limbo, unable to move on. He'd lost weight and wasn't sleeping well.

His friends worried about his melancholy. They told him to get a dog, so he adopted one of the Hurricane Andrew rescues. The staff told him the flat-coated retriever was bred to be a hunting dog with strong muscular jaws, but a soft mouth for retrieving game birds. The dog had webbed feet and possessed remarkable swimming ability. They called him Storm because of his ordeal in Florida.

Everyone loved Storm. His gregarious manner made women want to hug and mother him. His 70-pound body was lean with a wavy, coal-black coat. A long elegant neck gave him a regal bearing. His chocolate-brown eyes glistened through slightly loose, almond-shaped eyelids. Around people, his feathery tail wagged continuously. He didn't walk; he pranced, radiating joy with every step. The vet tech told Liam the flat-coated retriever has been labeled the Peter Pan dog, because they never seem to grow up. They retain their puppy playfulness throughout their lives. Storm might be just what he needed to make new friends, especially those of the opposite sex.

After an embarrassing squirrel-chasing incident in the local park, Liam enrolled his dog in an obedience class held at the scene of that transgression. Storm drew a lot of attention when his classmates learned about his hurricane survival. The flat-coat learned to sit, stay, and come when called… most of the time, as long as he believed they were playing a game. On more than one occasion, when the exercises became somewhat tedious, he broke loose and headed to the nearby pond for a swim with the ducks.

After completing obedience, Liam enrolled Storm in an agility training class. The teacher, Kathryn, and the other seven student-handlers were all women over fifty. The dogs ranged in size from miniature poodles to a pony-sized Newfoundland. Canine energy levels varied from comatose to frenzied. One lady called her Australian shepherd "Coriolis" because he spun in counterclockwise circles between obstacles like a low-pressure cyclone. Liam wondered if the earth's rotation would cause the dog to spin in the opposite direction in the southern hemisphere.

Kathryn was a regular encyclopedia of agility history. The sport began in England in the 1980s, she told the class. Dogs competed in activities similar to events normally reserved for horses. They ran courses with single, double, and triple jumps. The jump heights varied for small and large dogs. Negotiating weave poles like a slalom skier substituted for dressage. Animals darted through tunnels, leaped through tires and negotiated a teeter-totter. Carryover activities from obedience were invented. Dogs were trained to jump onto a table and lie down for a five-second count to show how well the handlers could control their pets. Some obstacles mimicked military skills, such as climbing an A-Frame and walking planks.

Kathryn insisted on lavishing prolific praise on the dogs with lots of food and toy rewards. The use of the word "no" was strictly forbidden. She admonished, "The brain is like Velcro for negative experiences, but Teflon for positive ones."

During the drills, the women with small dogs had a tendency to run bent at the waist, perhaps to keep a closer eye on their pet.

"BI-TO. Straighten up. You need to see where you're going," commanded Kathryn. "Those are searchlights, not metal detectors."

The terminology was a mystery to Liam, but when his turn came, he carefully maintained an upright posture. Toward the end of his turn, he bent down to see if his dog was correctly positioned to enter a tunnel.

Kathryn yelled, "BI-TO. Straighten up."

The rest of the class giggled. An elderly lady called out, "Kathryn, he doesn't have searchlights."

Liam looked a little embarrassed and stopped. "Would someone please tell me what BI-TO means?"

After a pause and a few more giggles, the elderly woman volunteered. "It's an acronym. Butt In. Boobs Out."

Liam looked puzzled. "Okay, I get the 'B-I' part, but instead of 'T-O", don't you mean 'B-O'?"

When he said 'B-O', the ladies all giggled. One student whispered to another, "He's so cute and don't you just love his dog?" She called out, "No one wants body odor. Think about it. Butt in, T- out. Searchlights. It'll come to you."

In a sudden moment of insight, Liam got it and blushed.

After a month's lessons, Kathryn told Liam that Storm was ready to compete, and suggested he enter the dog in an agility trial in Petaluma. Liam was so surprised he dropped Storm's leash, and the dog headed to the pond to get chummy with the ducks.

6   The Not So Perfect Storm

The rising sun temporarily blinded Liam as he drove into the parking lot at the Petaluma fairgrounds. After parking the car, he opened the cargo door. Storm wagged his tail furiously and grabbed a tennis ball out of the door pocket. His dark wet eyes sparkled, and his body wiggled in anticipation. Liam wished he could turn the dog loose and let him work off some energy, but he reluctantly snapped a leash onto his collar.

"Okay. Let's go."

The big retriever pulled hard on the leash as they moved toward a grassy area nearby.

"Easy!" Liam commanded. The dog pulled harder.

Storm snorted clouds of steamy vapor into the chilly morning air. He sniffed the first tree he came to and marked over the scent of a recent visitor. He squatted and completed stage two while still holding the tennis ball in his mouth. Liam pulled a plastic bag from his pocket. Neatness was important.

Liam hauled his shade canopy to a shady area. Several others had the same idea, and he was lucky to find the last clear spot to set up. A woman in the next space was putting the finishing touches on her canopy. He guessed she was about the same age as the ladies in the obedience and agility classes. She wore a white pullover wool hat and her smiling face reminded him of a full moon. A loose sweatshirt failed to disguise her lumpy body.

"Mind if I set up here?" he asked.

"Oh, please do. I'm Nora. You have that handsome black dog, don't you?"

"He's a flat-coated retriever. I'm Liam. What kind of dog do you have?"

"Moose is a papillon. That's French for butterfly. They're like toy spaniels with enormous ears."

He studied her little dog in a small soft crate under her canopy. "He's very cute."

She beamed. "Would you be a dear and help me with the last corner of my canopy? I can't quite reach that high."

Liam retrieved the errant end and pulled it over the aluminum frame.

"Oh, bless you," she said.

After setting up his trial equipment, Liam placed Storm in an ex-pen. He unfolded a deck chair, sat down, and ate his breakfast of doughnuts, washed down with a Pepsi. This would be his first dog agility trial. He tried not to think about the turmoil of the past year. His only contact with Myra had been when she stopped by the house to get clothes.

The spring sun climbed above the trees, and he began to relax as the temperature rose. He hadn't been sleeping well the past month and the warmth made him drowsy. He slumped down in his chair, but his neighbors' conversation prevented him from dozing.

Nora greeted a friend. "Mary Jo, good morning. You're running late today."

"Just as I'm getting ready to leave, my cat decides to throw up a hair ball," lamented Mary Jo.

"That's so disgusting, but it does make them feel better. I buy pet grass for my cat. It makes them throw up more often, but it's not so violent."

Mary Jo tilted her head to the right. "Wouldn't lawn grass be just as good?"

"You never know what might be on lawn grass."

Liam closed his eyes and attempted to resume his cat-nap. Perhaps you could stick your finger down her throat, he thought.

"How's your sheltie, Blazer, doing?" asked Nora.

"My little girl has two Standard qualifying runs and needs one more for her title. Her rear end seems a little stiff after workouts, so I've been using magnets to treat her."

"Magnets?"

"Yes, she wears a magnet pouch around the house on her little bottom to ease arthritis. I don't understand it, but it sure works. She used to knock bars down all the time, and now she's jumping so much better. We see the chiropractor once a month for an adjustment, and of course she gets acupuncture. It's made all the difference."

Liam smiled. He imagined the Sheltie running around with a magnet pouch hanging on her rear end.

The ladies moved on, and Liam drifted in and out of slumber. He slid further down in his chair, resting his head on the backrest. The agility trial that day had replaced his usual morning run. Now he dreamed he was running on a beach along the edge of the water. Others joined him, and they continued running barefoot, splashing though the shallow surf in perfect unison. He had trouble keeping up and fell behind.

Nora's excited voice jolted him awake. "I'm sorry to bother you, but there's a problem in the women's bathroom. No one can use the stall because a frog's sitting on the toilet. Could you remove that creepy thing?"

Liam, now fully awake, forced a smile. "I think I can do that."

"Oh, bless you."

After the restroom was verified vacant, Liam entered. Sure enough, the largest amphibian he'd ever seen sat on the commode, apparently sleeping. It had dry, leathery brown skin covered with wart-like glands. He picked up the interloper and triumphantly emerged to a hearty round of applause from a small group of women.

He smiled, something he needed to do more often these days. "Actually, it's a toad. If one of you gave him a kiss, he might turn into a prince."

The ladies tittered. All that day, strangers gave him bemused thanks for clearing the restroom.

Liam waited for the first course to be set. He reached over the side of the ex-pen and stroked Storm's neck and back. The contact had a calming effect on both man and dog as they waited for the first competition.

He watched Nora and her papillon prepare for their turn in the ring. Moose moved from tree to tree, sometimes lifting his left leg and at other times his right. He never seemed to run dry. After each encounter, the tiny dog did a fierce chicken scratch with all four legs, sending his scent to as wide an area as possible. He growled as he scratched, making sure to be heard by any other dogs close by.

When the first event was ready, Liam walked the course with the other handlers. He needed to memorize the sequence of obstacles and plan his strategy to negotiate the course correctly. A rubber pylon numbered each obstacle. He was especially apprehensive about obstacle eight, the four-foot high, thirty-six foot long dog walk. The dogs were required to touch the forty-two-inch yellow zones at the base of the ascending and descending planks. This had been a problem for his long-striding dog in the agility classes.

Fifty handlers moved intently around the course, practicing their skills. The whole process reminded Liam of a movie he'd seen about zombies. Every now and then one of them would stop, extend an arm, and mumble, "Contact, go tunnel, scramble, go hup." A few handlers began racing around at full speed, seemingly oblivious of the others. By some miracle, no collisions took place. Some practiced their movements, extending their arms while making swooping movements as if they were pretending to be airplanes, while muttering imaginary commands.

Liam wondered if the CIA could use the agility trial walk-through to convince hostile aliens that our planet has no intelligent life worth destroying.

A whistle woke the zombies. Everyone crowded around Judge Preston Wadsworth. Two weeks earlier, Liam had watched a trial with his classmates and saw the judge compete with Ringo, a powerful Australian shepherd. Preston was tall, lean, and handsome, like Myra's present male companion. He was always in complete control. As a team, he and the dog had seemed to be attached by an invisible cord while they competed. They were the only team that regularly beat the border collies, whose speed often got them into trouble. Liam enjoyed the crazy antics of the speedy collies. They reminded him of devil-may-care downhill racers in skiing. He remembered racecar driver Mario Andretti's quote: "If you feel like you are in control, then you aren't going fast enough."

Because Preston was judging, he could not compete on this day. When all the handlers were assembled, he began his briefing. "The yardage today is 185 yards, and you'll have 58 seconds to complete the course. We have a lot of dogs trialing today and want to finish before dark. If you hear my whistle, you're eliminated. Please get off the course as fast as possible. Good luck. Run fast and run clean."

Liam watched the competition begin. Storm whimpered, anxious to have his turn. Many dogs were eliminated. Upset handlers grumbled about being whistled off before they were done. "We paid our money. At least let us finish the course," lamented one. Only the Velcro dogs were succeeding. They stuck close to their handlers and turned promptly on command. Border collies, in particular, were having great difficulty. The contorted, twisting course required close contact with their handlers. As herding dogs, they readily moved away from their handlers and worked better at a distance.

Eventually, it was Storm's turn. He wagged his tail so vigorously that his whole body gyrated. "Stay," Liam commanded and moved off the start line. As he pivoted at the first obstacle, he caught sight of a black blur moving past him. Storm had broken his start line stay. By some miracle, he negotiated the first three obstacles correctly. He ripped through a tunnel and headed for the A-frame.

"Scramble," Liam commanded. So far, so good. Two more jumps were cleanly done. The big dog thundered toward the dog walk.

"Easy." Liam attempted to slow his dog, who often launched over the yellow zones if he moved too fast. The missed contact drew a penalty of ten faults. Storm headed for a tunnel under the dog walk. Liam stopped quickly, his feet slipped, and he landed hard on his tailbone. Storm ducked into the tunnel. Off course. Elimination. The sound of a whistle pierced the Petaluma stillness. Preston slid his left hand across his throat, like he was committing a murderous ritual, the signal for elimination. Meanwhile, Storm grabbed rubber pylon number eight in his mouth and began running around the ring in a big circle. The crowd laughed, but not Preston.

"Please take control of your dog and leave the ring."

Liam struggled to his feet and rescued pylon number eight.

Preston blew his whistle again, a little louder and longer. "You're eliminated. Leave the course."

"That's the man who got the frog out of the restroom," came a voice from the crowd, amid a smattering of applause. Liam hurried to the finish and leashed Storm, who put his front feet on his handler's chest and licked his face. Liam rubbed his tailbone, which was smarting. As he led his errant dog away from the ring, the retriever lunged toward a doughnut held carelessly by a spectator, who saved it in the nick of time.

Liam felt slightly embarrassed, but chuckled as he relived his dog's antics in the ring. Screw you, Preston, he thought. That's the most fun I've had in a while.

"Are you okay?" asked Nora.

"I landed on my tailbone. I'll be all right."

"I could rub it with my magnet," Mary Jo offered in sympathy.

After a pause, Liam said, "Come on, Mary Jo. I never hit on you."

They all giggled like teenagers.

The trial lasted until six that evening. Two different courses produced no qualifying runs, although one was close. Nora swore that Storm had touched the yellow zone on the dog walk, albeit barely, but Preston whistled him off the course. During the afternoon, several competitors came up to Liam and commented, "Such a handsome dog. We love his spirit."

On the way home, Liam ordered from the super-size menu at Burgers to Go. That night Storm jumped up on the bed. Liam dreamed he was running along a forest trail. He passed a group of runners. His stride was relaxed and strong with no weariness.

7 The Alpha Female[1]

The coastal morning fog draped the Monterrey Peninsula, shielding it from the relative sameness of the nearby Salinas valley. A fortuitous break in the mist helped Liam find the entrance to Carmel Regional Park, the site of the El Monte Kennel Club agility trial. After parking, Liam walked Storm to a grassy area near the parking lot, where the dog quickly relieved himself.

"Be sure to stoop and scoop," came the voice of a rotund, middle-aged woman standing nearby. The woman's short gray hair was partly hidden by a large straw hat. She wore spotless white tennis shoes and a floral print dress. The usual attire for women whose dogs competed in this sport was much more casual. Resisting his initial annoyance at being treated like a school child, Liam pulled a plastic bag from his pocket and gently waved it.

"Thank you," she replied. "Remember, your dog must be on leash at all times. Is that a flat-coat?"

"Yeah, he's a flatie. You know your dogs. I got him from a shelter. He didn't have registry papers, so he's been ILP'd."

---

[1]Wolves are social animals. They live in groups with a definite hierarchy. Animal behaviorists designate the leaders of the pack as alpha males and alpha females. These feed first, and maintain their dominance by posturing, staring, and other actions, such as urine marking.

"He's so handsome. I'll bet he could have been a show champion. It's a shame you had to neuter him to get him registered. Non-registered dogs aren't allowed at the trial site, you know."

"You here for the trial?" Liam asked.

The woman looked surprised. "Yes. Looks like this fog is lifting, and it's going to be a glorious day." She took a small black bag from the trunk of her car. Liam noticed she didn't have the paraphernalia most people bring to a trial.

Because she liked his dog, Liam's image of her as a despotic schoolteacher dissipated. "Can I help you carry anything?"

"That's very thoughtful, but this is all I have. Good luck today."

The trial ring looked as if Martha Stewart had organized it. The equipment was painted pastel pink and yellow. Vases of yellow, white, and pink mums were displayed on the check-in tables. All the officials wore bright orange blazers and white-brimmed hats. The casual observer would have had great difficulty singling out a Caltrans worker in this colorful setting.

Liam had already discovered that women dominate agility trials. They do the planning, set the local ground rules, and relish controlling the paperwork required to run the events. Men are tolerated because they help haul heavy equipment from place to place. At this trial, men numbered fewer than ten percent. Liam had to keep an eye out when using the men's restroom. The overflow from the crowded ladies' room often spilled in that direction.

He proceeded to the check-in table in and received a stuffed animal, two pieces of peppermint candy, and a dog bone, reminding him of the favors girls got at dances twenty years before when he was in college. His armband displayed Storm's number for the day: 24-23. Decoded, that meant he would jump hurdles twenty-four inches high and be twenty-third in the order of dogs running at that height.

The dogs would be jumping hurdles, dashing through tunnels, climbing A-Frames and seesaws, and negotiating weave poles like slalom skiers. The pink dog walk consisted of three connecting planks, each twelve feet long and a foot wide. The up and down planks had yellow areas at their bases called contact zones that the dogs had to touch as they left the apparatus. The center plank was four feet above the grass. Touching the yellow zones would be a real challenge.

In the center of the course was a two-foot high table with a three-foot square top. The excited dogs, after jumping hurdles and racing through tunnels, would be required to jump onto the table, stop dead, and lie down for five seconds. Liam appreciated the discipline required. He imagined ten-year-old children being told to suddenly stop and lie down for a count of five after chasing each other around a playground.

Promptly at seven-thirty, the handlers entered the course area without their dogs to memorize the sequence of obstacles and plan their strategy. After obstacle number ten the dogs were required to clear a hurdle and make a ninety-degree turn to the table. Liam grimaced when he saw the nightmare maneuver. If a dog had too much speed, it would race past the table and get a refusal penalty. Liam was standing near the table, contemplating this problem, when he was nearly knocked to the ground by a pretty young woman who had been bobbing around the course choreographing her moves as if she were dancing a Vienna waltz.

"Oh, I'm terribly sorry," she said.

"That's okay. I shouldn't stand in a major traffic area. I'm trying to figure out how to get my dog on this table without a refusal."

Her armband read 20-15, so Liam assumed her dog would jump twenty-inch hurdles. "Oh, my God. I know what you mean, and we've got the judge from hell today."

"Really?"

"Excuse my French, but she's a real witch."

"How's that?"

"Oh, I've seen her before. She's all business. She really relishes raising her hands and calling faults. When she designs these courses, she takes weeks figuring out how to screw us up. I need only one more qualifying round for my Aussie to get his MX."

Liam recalled Kathryn telling him that an MX title was the doggie equivalent of a college Master's degree. Another course walker motioned them to get out of the way, so they stepped back a few yards and 20-15 continued, "My ten-year-old daughter, Tiffany, is here today. We made a deal. She got her ears pierced and promised to come with Mommy today." She gestured toward a young girl outside the ring. Tiffany was dancing, imitating the latest Disney tween queen pictured on her T-shirt. "So this morning we're waiting to use the ladies' restroom, and the line is so long. Tiffany's doing a little dance, she has to go so bad. I wanted to use the men's room, but Tiff refused. Well, the judge comes over and just goes to the front of the line. She says, 'Excuse me, but I'm in a hurry.' I was like so totally freaked out."

20-15 reminded Liam of his competitive ex-wife, who sold real estate in the style of Donald Trump. She liked glitz, was high maintenance, and a chain smoker. Liam, on the other hand, enjoyed sweating through a four-mile run, followed by a nap or an afternoon watching the 49ers.

"Did anyone protest?" he said.

"Are you kidding? She's the judge. I wanted to give her a really mean stare, but I was afraid she'd get even."

"You mean, call faults that didn't happen?"

"Well, she sure wouldn't give us a break."

The announcement came to assemble for the judge's briefing. Liam recognized the judge as the woman in the straw hat and white tennis shoes that he'd met in the parking lot.

"Good morning, everyone. I'm Helen Pickering-Meeks."

"Good morning," came the muted reply by a few.

Liam admired women with hyphenated names. If he were in their married tennis shoes, he'd resist losing his last name, especially if the acquired surname was Meeks. Helen didn't appear meek.

Helen winced in feigned pain, reminding Liam of his fourth-grade teacher, Miss Krause. "Let's try that again. Good morning!"

"Good morning," came the louder apathetic reply.

Helen forced a smile. "That's better. I'm sure you all know the rules. I want to see everyone on the line ready to go when their turn comes. No wasted time. We want to finish at a decent hour. I've got a plane to catch this evening, and I'll never make it unless we keep this trial moving."

She stopped and stared at two women who had slipped away and were walking the course. "You two. Stop! Come back here. I'm not done yet."

The two women, red-faced, slunk back to the group.

"Now, please feel free to ask any questions."

One timid woman said, "Is it a fault if my dog hits a jump bar and it wiggles around, but doesn't fall off for a few seconds?"

"Section 17 in your rule book covers that. Yes, five faults. Don't make the judge think. Just perform so there's no question you've done everything correctly. I don't like sloppy performances. Any other questions?" Helen paused five seconds and announced, "I want the first dog on the line in two minutes."

As Liam waited his turn, he massaged the soft black fur on Storm's neck. 20-15 waited nearby with her handsome blue merle Australian shepherd. The solid-looking Aussie was black with patches of bluish-gray fur. A white blaze on the muzzle was a striking contrast to his blue eyes and black nose. Aussies have been bred for their toughness and are fearless herding dogs.

Liam saw Tiffany standing quietly nearby. Her plastic earrings, miniature blue merle Aussies, dangled from her newly pierced ear lobes.

"Mom, can I have a dog?"

"Tiff, we already have a dog."

"He's really your dog. I want one of my own, like that black dog over there."

Liam smiled. The fun-loving Tiffany and a flat-coat would make a good pair.

"When you get older, we'll consider it. Maybe another Aussie. Don't you want a dog that can win?"

Tiffany fingered her earrings. "I guess."

The trial proceeded. Handlers approached the starting line like Christians facing lions in the Coliseum. They were tense. Some left in tears. No one was qualifying. Agility trials were usually fun. People smile and laugh, even if their dogs act goofy in the ring. But smiles at this trial were about as common as rock musicians who just say no.

As Liam predicted, the approach to the table produced refusals for many fast dogs. 20-15's dog had a perfect run in progress, but she started celebrating before her dog reached the finish. She raised her arms and screamed in joy. Her dog turned to look at her and knocked a bar down on the last obstacle. Disqualified. 20-15 fell to her knees in anguish.

The course was reset for the Novice dogs. Liam waited near the entrance gate. When 24-22 finished, he hurried into the competition ring.

"Excuse me, 24-23," yelled the gate steward in her spiffy orange blazer. "You can't go into the ring yet. They're resetting a bar. I'll tell you when you can enter."

"I'm sorry." Liam quickly exited and waited until the course was ready. Helen nodded at him, so he entered the ring again.

"Excuse me, I didn't say you could go in yet," the gate steward admonished him.

Judge Helen walked over to the steward and gave her a look Miss Krause would have been proud of. "Young lady, I appreciate your dedication to your duty, but if we wish to finish this trial before the next millennium, please allow this man immediate access to my ring."

Everyone involved in the day's activity was getting a little rattled. Liam led Storm to the start line, removed his slip-on leash, and dropped it behind him. The leash would be at the finish line because the leash runner would carry it there from the start line while the dog was running the course.

Storm's run proceeded precariously. Every obstacle was taken on the brink of disaster. Several times the flat-coat came within an eyelash of taking the wrong obstacle.

Liam struggled to keep control. He stopped dead in his tracks and shouted for his runaway dog to stay on the proper path. He used body language to direct left or right turns as he delivered commands. "Out. Jump. Go on." Some dogs were described as "soft." If their handler made harsh corrections, they might quit. Storm was anything but soft. He had only two modes: full throttle and sleeping.

Halfway through the course, still with no faults, they approached the dreaded table sequence. Liam froze, speechless. As Storm jumped the hurdle before the table, he circled back with no refusal, leaped onto the table, and slid across scratching frantically with his claws trying to stop. At the last instant, he caught his nails near the edge to avoid falling off. He stood at attention, his tongue hanging out the side of his mouth, his dark brown eyes wide open and wild looking.

Liam finally got his voice back. "Lie down!" Storm collapsed immediately into a perfect down on the table. Judge Helen counted, "Five, four, three." Liam detected the hint of a smile. Was she thinking this was a dog that could meet the challenge of her course from hell?

"Two, one, go!"

The next sequence was successful. Only the dog walk and one hurdle remained. Liam halted as they approached the up plank. Hopefully, that would slow his dog enough so he'd get a foot in the contact zones. Storm slowed, but leaped off the down plank well short of touching the yellow. This meant that, after his marvelous run, he would not qualify. He raced to the last hurdle, but had to dodge the runner who was late transporting his leash.

Liam glanced at the judge. Her tortured face rekindled memories of Miss Krause the day Billy Sue Montgomery threw up during the Thanksgiving Pageant. Helen blew her whistle so loudly that spectators grimaced and held their ears. Nearby dogs howled. She bellowed. "The leash runner has interfered with this run. 24-23 will get a rerun."

Liam swore he felt a sudden breeze as the spectators gasped. Helen Pickering-Meeks was giving someone a break.

The rerun was worse than the initial run. Storm missed the yellow zone on the dog walk, and got a refusal at the table. When it was over, Liam glanced sheepishly at Helen. He may have misread her, but she looked disappointed.

The fog lifted. The sun came out, and it was a glorious day. At midday, Helen proceeded to the front of the lunch line, as well as the rest room line. After all, she was very busy that day. That was the last straw for 20-15, who packed up and left. Liam hoped Tiffany would get her own dog, one that wasn't high maintenance, one that liked to jump up on the sofa to take naps or run the trails just for fun.

The story of that day passed into agility folklore. Liam overheard stories saying that Storm qualified. Some said he won the event. Eventually, he stopped correcting those embellished accounts.

Newcomers sneered in disbelief. "Helen Pickering-Meeks gave a rerun? Impossible."

8 The Visitor

On her first day at her new home, Ben Kowalski's newly adopted shelter dog froze in position and stared into a shrub. A brown towhee flew out, trying to gain altitude in the last flight of its life. The dog snapped the bird out of the air and gave it one quick shake before the lifeless bird fell to the ground.

Ben was mortified. "Myst, no!"

The dog hung her head and her tail dropped between her legs, but her bird hunting ended that day and never occurred again. Ben felt bad yelling at his dog, but there had to be limits.

The next morning Ben was sitting in the patio, playing fetch with Myst. She could retrieve a tennis ball and dump it in his lap almost before his arm came down. During lulls in the fetch game, she would trot back and forth across the lawn, now and then bouncing into the air to snap at a gnat or some unseen flying critter. Myst wouldn't quit, so after a dozen retrievals, Ben stopped the game. The temperature had already climbed into the eighties. The sprinklers left puddles along the fence, and the dog lay down in the mud to cool her belly.

Ben told Myst to sit and, to his surprise, she did so instantly. "Lie down," he ordered. The border collie responded immediately. It was clear she had received training from a previous owner. Why would someone train a dog, and then dump it one night at the animal shelter?

When Ben walked from room to room, he heard the click-click of the dog's nails as she followed him. If he sat down, she turned a few circles and curled up nearby. At night, she waited a short time before she jumped quietly onto Ben's bed, curling up at his feet. He didn't have the heart to push her off. There was something comforting about the devotion of this dog.

Early one evening, Myst lay sleeping on the carpet nearby. Ben gazed out the living room window. Century-old shade trees dotted his lawn of plush Kentucky bluegrass. A white picket fence, badly in need of paint, bordered the perimeter. Scrub jays and finches worked the bird feeders. Every fall, the jays raided his apple tree, and it still produced enough fruit for the entire block. He even managed to save a large bag of apples to drop off at the senior center.

A grimy old Datsun drove slowly by his home, its second trip in the last twenty minutes. Traffic in this quiet neighborhood was sporadic at best, and Ben was tempted to write down the license number, or call the police until he saw the driver was a young woman. Maybe she was lost.

The Datsun parked on the street in front of his house, its windshield streaked with the corpses of insects smeared by worn-out wiper blades. Boxes and piles of clothes filled the back seat. The driver got out and stretched her arms over her head. Ben guessed she'd been driving for some time. She paused for a moment and glanced at the street number stenciled on the curb. She moved her head to one side, flipped her shoulder length auburn hair from her eyes, and walked slowly up his sidewalk to the front door. Her filmy dress accentuated her thinness, reminding Ben of Rebecca before they were married.

Ben wouldn't usually open the door to strangers or solicitors, but the woman who rang the doorbell didn't fit that pattern.

Myst, now fully awake, ran to the door. After waiting for several seconds and getting no response, the visitor turned and started to leave. If she had rung a second time, Ben surely would have ignored her – he didn't like pushy people – but curiosity overcame him. He told the dog to stay and opened the door. "Can I help you?"

The woman, halfway down the sidewalk, stopped and turned back. "Oh, I'm sorry to bother you. Would you happen to know a Mrs. Kowalski? I wanted to say hello."

"Mrs. Kowalski passed away recently."

The young woman nodded. "I'm so sorry. I didn't know."

He took a long breath. "Were you one of her students?"

"Yes. She was my favorite teacher."

"We were married forty-five years." A flood of memories cascaded in Ben's brain. He didn't warm to strangers, but felt his guard evaporating. "Won't you come in? Can I get you something to drink?"

"Well, thank you, but I really need to get going."

"You look like you've been driving a while and could use a break."

"Okay, how about a glass of water? My name is Cassidy O'Neal. Please call me Cassy."

Ben was stunned. So this was girl Rebecca had told him about as her life ebbed away. He brought her a glass of water, and they sat in the living room. Myst lay at Ben's feet, staring intently at their guest.

Cassy smiled. "That's a pretty dog. Border collie, isn't she?"

"You know your dogs. Her name's Myst."

"I lived on a farm for a while. We had dogs like that."

Ben recalled his wife's story. Cassy and her mother had lived in New Mexico before coming to Northern California. He tried not to stare at his mesmerizing guest and shifted his gaze from time to time. "Rebecca told me you were one of her favorite students."

Cassy feigned agreement. "Oh, sure. I bet. I cut class, didn't do my homework, and wrote notes in class. One day, I came to school with purple hair. The dean stopped me in the hallway and wanted to send me home, but they didn't have that rule then, so she sent me back to your wife's English class. 'Hi, Cassy, I like your hair,' your wife said."

Ben wouldn't normally share personal information, but responded. "Did you notice my wife had a blond streak in her hair? I think she used peroxide. She dyed the rest of her hair to hide the gray."

"I noticed. I thought she was pretty cool. So then your wife said, 'Cassy, you're such a pretty girl. Why don't you cut your hair so you have bangs?' So I did, and the next day I know she noticed, but didn't say anything. She just smiled at me. You know, I didn't cut her class the rest of the year, and I pulled up my grade from a C to an A. I wouldn't have gone to Sonoma State if she didn't help me get a scholarship."

Ben agreed. "That gave her a lot of satisfaction."

"I really should get going. I drove down from Eureka. I was going to stay with my mom, but when I stopped by her house today, I found out she moved to Alaska. We haven't been in touch for a while."

"Where to next?"

Cassy paused a moment. "I'm going to look up some high school friends. Maybe bum a few nights with someone."

"You don't sound confident about that plan."

"It's been several years since I graduated. Most of my friends are married or have moved away."

"So you drove from Eureka today?"

"Yesterday."

"If you don't mind me asking a personal question, where did you stay last night?"

"Well, I got down here so late, I just slept in the car. I don't usually do that. It's not like I'm homeless."

Many baffling questions about Cassy O'Neal disturbed Ben. "Look, nobody should be sleeping in a car. It's too dangerous, especially for a young woman like you. Tell you what. It's getting late. If you like, you can spend the night here. Get a good night's rest, and tomorrow—"

"Oh, I couldn't do that. I don't want to put you to any trouble."

"No trouble. I insist. Perhaps you can walk the dog. I have a little trouble getting around these days."

"Are you sure? Her name's Myst, right?"

Upon hearing her name, the dog jumped to her feet, trotted across the room, and put her head in the visitor's lap.

9   Morning Vision

On a warm October morning at the Santa Rosa Fairgrounds, Liam waited for the Halloween weekend agility competition to begin. He adjusted his San Francisco Giants baseball cap to block the sun, and slouched lazily in his lawn chair, drifting in and out of an early morning slumber. As his head started to fall back, he jerked upright and opened his eyes. For a moment he thought he was still dreaming. A young woman strolled casually on the other side of the field, between him and the low sun. Rays of light passed through her knee-length dress, silhouetting her willowy figure. She tossed her head carelessly to one side, realigning the sunlight venting through her hair. She and her dog had a lightness to their steps, as though they moved in slow motion. They passed behind a canopy and disappeared.

Fully awake now, Liam searched the sea of blue and teal canopies, lawn chairs, and the array of nervous handlers getting their dogs ready for the competition. Had he imagined that apparition?

Out of the corner of his eye, she appeared again on his right, gliding toward Liam past the pens of other dogs. She was the only woman in this legion of canine athletes and human athlete wannabes wearing a dress, and the only one who was barefoot. Perhaps thirty years old, her dress swayed from side to side in slow motion as she approached. Her medium-sized dog had a black body, white mane, and white feet.

The woman spotted Storm before noticing Liam slouched in the lawn chair. Their eyes met. Liam looked away, a little embarrassed to be caught staring so intently.

The woman smiled. "Is that a Labrador retriever?"

Liam straightened up in his chair. His voice still had its early morning huskiness. He tried not to sound like a dog-matic classroom teacher, but failed. "Actually, a flat-coated retriever."

The woman's smile broadened. "He looks so friendly. Can I pet him?"

"Sure. He has a tendency to get carried away. Be careful he doesn't butt you in the mouth."

Storm picked up a tennis ball and put his front feet on the sides of the ex-pen. His tail wagged violently as he greeted a new friend. His black body and orange collar made him look like a little boy preparing to trick-or-treat. Her dog backed up and growled.

Liam gaped at the alluring stranger as she petted Storm. Her shoulder-length hair turned slightly inward at her neck, and her fair skin was the prefect match for sparkling green eyes. He knew her dog's breed, but in a feeble attempt to make conversation asked, "Is your dog a border collie?"

"Yes, I'm walking her for a friend of mine. She's quite shy. I'm trying to socialize her. Her name's Myst."

Liam stood and took a step toward Myst, who barked and scurried to the woman's side. He plucked the tennis ball from Storm's mouth and immediately got the collie's attention. He rolled the ball a few feet. She quickly retrieved it and dropped it at his feet. Storm whimpered and pounded on his pen with his front paws.

The woman looked pleased. "She's usually suspicious of strangers, especially men."

"Would you like to take our dogs to a corner of the field and let them run a little?" he asked.

"Why not?" she said.

"I'm Liam."

"Cassy."

Away from the competition's hubbub, Liam threw balls for both dogs. Myst watched intensely each time he reared back to throw. Her legs bent, she accelerated to full speed in two steps. He tried to fool her, as he often did with Storm by not throwing the ball, but she would wheel around, ready to sprint in any direction. She barely touched the ground and could change direction in an eye blink.

"They're like children, aren't they?" Cassy said.

Liam glanced at her left hand and saw she was not wearing a ring. "For some of the people here, the dogs are their children." After an awkward pause, he said, "Do you live nearby?"

Cassy pushed her hair to one side. "I'm staying with this wonderful old man in Sebastopol. He married my favorite high school teacher. She passed away, and I think he's lonely. I didn't have a place to stay, so he said I could stay with him. Myst is his dog."

"That was nice of him."

"I really can't explain it. I was such a bitch in high school, but his wife kept encouraging me to make something of myself. I never would have gone to college without her help."

"Where'd you go?"

"Sonoma State. Mom lived in Cotati, and it was close. I loved the free spirit environment."

Liam nodded. "I took a summer class there a few years ago. I was surprised to see marijuana growing in the flower-beds at the residence hall. Did you grow up in this area?"

"Mom said the whole scene in the sixties got to be too much for her, so she moved to a farm in New Mexico. When I was real young, I remember this black and white dog, like Myst, herding a group of ducks around just for the hell of it."

"So you grew up on a farm."

"People called it a commune. Several families lived and worked together. Eventually, they got on each other's nerves and split. We moved to Cotati when I started high school."

Storm dropped the ball about three feet from Cassy and tapped his feet, wagged his tail furiously, and stared at the ball.

Cassy reared back and sent the ball flying. "What do you do, Liam?"

"Science teacher at Sonoma Central High."

"That must be satisfying."

"It has its ups and downs." Something about this pretty young woman made Liam feel at ease, yet he sensed a vulnerability that made him want to know more. "May I ask why you came today?"

"I saw a story in the newspaper about this event. The old gentleman really can't take care of his dog. She's shy and has so much energy. I walk her, but she needs more exercise. To tell the truth, it's been a little boring since I moved from Eureka. I was a waitress and…promise you won't laugh?"

"I'll try."

"Mom was always protesting something: the war, nuclear facilities in Livermore, a San Francisco freeway…I had some time, so I camped out with a group who tried to halt the cutting down of old growth redwood trees."

"I remember seeing the news clips."

"They talked me into living in a giant old tree to help support their cause."

Liam paused and rubbed his eyes a moment. "Are you putting me on?"

"I felt I had to do something. Thousand-year-old trees were being cut down to make fences."

Liam grinned. "Living in a tree? I mean how did you…"

"Go to the bathroom? Don't ask." Cassy laughed. "It rained every day. It was miserable, but looking back, I'd do it again."

"I admire your conviction."

"The nights were cold and foggy, but occasionally the sky would clear. The stars and the moon were so beautiful. My code name was Moonbeam. I wanted to be the first woman to walk on the moon."

"I won't tell you what some of my students call me!"

Cassy laughed again. "You'll have to tell me sometime."

Liam felt a little rusty picking up clues from pretty young women, but it sounded like she wanted to meet him again. "Storm's turn in the ring is coming up. Would you like to watch?"

"Sure. Looks like fun. Could you tell me how to get started?"

"No problem. Wait until I get back."

Liam felt an adrenaline rush as he approached the ring.

Storm spotted a little girl sitting on the ground and licked her face as they passed.

"Ahhhk," she shrieked, more excited than frightened, wiping her face.

"Sorry," Liam said.

Liam and Storm entered the ring. He glanced across the field to confirm that Cassy was watching. He told Storm to stay and moved onto the course. He half expected Storm to break prematurely, but Storm remained rock solid behind the start line. He was the biggest dog competing that day, and the spectators watched in awe as Liam released the flat-coat, who thundered around the course, through tunnels, through the weave poles, over an A-frame, up and down the seesaw, and through the tire jump. Storm leaped up onto the dog walk at a full gallop. It shuddered when he raced across and down. He cleared the final jump and sprinted past the finish line. It was the first time they had ever completed a course with no faults.

Storm paused, wagging his tail, his tongue hanging several inches out of the left side of his mouth. Liam attempted to leash him, but he bolted, jumped the three-foot high barrier marking the boundary of the ring, and ran directly to where Cassy had been standing. Liam ran to Storm and leashed him. He looked for her, but she was gone.

10 Forest Gumption

Cassy glanced in the rear-view mirror. She thought she'd seen a former boyfriend's truck in the Petaluma parking lot. She felt badly that she had bolted from the agility trial without a word to Liam, but was afraid she was being followed.

After graduating from Sonoma State, she'd drifted from job to job and ended up unemployed. When her money ran out, she and her high school pal, Claire, drove up the north coast. They camped in the Humboldt Redwoods State Park for a few days to keep expenses down, then found waitress jobs at Buster's Bar and Grill near Eureka.

They were pretty clever at fending off amorous drunken lumbermen, but something about the guitar player in a run of the mill local band intrigued Cassy. Frank seemed to be a little smarter than the average bar clientele. He had a head for business and made lots of money in an area that was financially depressed. He told her he wanted to save the old growth redwoods…at least, those in the backwoods area where he liked to spend time.

Later, Cassy learned the real reason for Frank's conservation concerns. Lumbering in the local forest was likely to expose his hemp crop. She had nothing against marijuana, and indeed had spent some weekends in high school stoned, but she resented Frank's deception, not to mention his quick temper. She broke off the relationship, but he continued to pester her.

Out of frustration, Cassy traveled to the Owl Creek Redwood Grove and volunteered, along with several others, to camp on platforms in old growth trees to prevent them from being logged. It wasn't long before she realized that was a bad idea, even though Claire smuggled her a six-pack of beer every now and then. To make matters worse, it rained almost every day, but at least Frank had stopped bothering her.

She settled into a routine. She had a cell phone and tried to read a book a day. She plugged the leaks in her makeshift tarp shelter. The food hoisted to her every couple days got better. She thought about her life and how it had been wasted up to that point. She wanted to get her act together and not end up like her mother.

After one month, five days, and twenty-one hours, Cassy came down from her tree. She'd heard Frank's "farm" had been discovered, and he was in jail. She drove back to Sonoma County, hoping to get her life on the right track. Deeply saddened by the news of Mrs. Kowalski's passing, she accepted Ben's offer to stay with him. Her only other option was spending another night in her Datsun.

At five o'clock Cassy's car pulled into the driveway. Myst jumped out, ran to the door, and greeted her owner. Ben smiled broadly as the collie placed her front legs on him and tried in vain to plant wet kisses on his face.

"Hi, strangers! I was afraid you had car trouble."

"Sorry we took so long. We had a blast today. We watched dogs jumping through tires, climbing A-frames, and all kinds of things."

"The hell you say."

"I'd like to try that with Myst, if it's all right with you."

"Sure, we have a big yard. By the way, someone came by to see you today. Said his name was Frank, and he'd come back later."

Cassy lost her smile. "Oh God!"

"Something wrong?"

"Oh, he was this loser I knew in Eureka." *Why did she always get mixed up with the wrong guy?*

"If he comes back, should I say you don't want to see him?"

"Thanks, but it probably won't do any good. I'll take care of it." Cassy tried to remain unconcerned. No sense in getting Ben involved. "I met this guy today at the Fairgrounds, a teacher, but I couldn't stay because…something came up."

Ben looked concerned. "What's that?"

"Oh, it's probably nothing. I thought I saw someone I didn't want to deal with. Maybe I'm getting a little paranoid. It was nothing."

Cassy prepared dinner and finished cleaning the kitchen while Ben dozed through the evening news on TV. She was disturbed by the day's events. How had Frank found her?

A little past seven, she saw a beat-up Ford truck pull up in front of the house. She took a deep breath and walked outside, closing the door quietly behind her. If she could handle drunken lumbermen, she could handle this.

Frank started up the walk. He looked like he hadn't shaved in several days, but with his long hair and earrings, he still had his rock star good looks.

"Hi, baby. I had some business down this way and thought I'd look you up. I've missed you."

"How did you know I'd be here?"

"You always talked about that teacher of yours. There's only one Kowalski in the local phone book. Look, I'd like to try again. Give me another chance."

"Did you follow me this morning?"

"Now, why would I do that?"

"We've been through this before. It's over. My life is taking a new direction."

"I'm not growing weed anymore. I'm pretty handy at fixing things. I'm going to open a repair shop."

"I heard your field was discovered."

"Yeah, aerial photographs."

"You didn't tell me you were growing pot when we met."

Frank shrugged his shoulders. "I'm sorry. Let bygones be bygones. That's my motto."

"And you did time in the slammer."

"They had to let me go. The narcs couldn't prove it was my field."

"It's over, Frank."

"Dammit. Gimme a break. I told you I was sorry!"

Cassy held up her hand. "Hold it down. Mr. Kowalski is sleeping."

"Don't tell me to shut up."

"I didn't tell you to shut up. I asked you to keep your voice down."

"Look, Cassy, I came here real friendly like, and you treat me like some poor cousin. I didn't drive down here to get the brushoff."

"I think you'd better go now."

"Screw you. I'll leave when I feel like it."

Just then, Ben opened the door, with Myst a step behind. He moved directly toward the visitor, stopping a yard away. "Young man, we'd like you leave."

"You old fart. What are you going to do about it?"

The old man's face flushed, and his eyes grew steely. His breathing was labored. "If I were younger, I'd kick your ass."

"You and who else?"

Ben picked up his cane and waved it in a circle above his head. "You son-of-a-bitch. Get off my property."

Cassy stepped between the two men. "Please leave or I'm calling the police," she told Frank.

"I'm leaving, but you haven't heard the last of me. I'll be back." Frank stormed to his truck and gunned the engine, leaving rubber tire marks on the street as he screeched away. The truck careened around the corner and disappeared.

Cassy helped Ben into the house and guided him to a chair. He was sweating, his skin clammy to her touch. He tried to catch his breath.

"Are you okay?" she asked, worried.

He couldn't answer. She saw the frightened look in his eyes.

"Oh, my God. I'm calling 911."

Ben clasped his hands hard to his chest, and his head rolled forward.

11 The Secret

At eight o'clock the next morning, the doctor at the hospital briefed Cassy. "It looks like a coronary occlusion. We're using anticoagulants. So far they seem to be working. Please keep your visit down to ten minutes."

Cassy was relieved that her prompt action had helped. Ben looked tired and smiled weakly when she entered his room. Oxygen tubes exited his nostrils, and an IV was attached to one arm. He was hooked up to screen that monitored his EKG, producing high-pitched beeps that continually broke the silence.

"How's Myst?" he asked.

"She's been moping around all morning. She's fine, but she misses you."

"Thanks for taking care of her."

"The doctor says you're doing better. I can't tell you how scared I was."

"You know what one of my pills is? Aspirin. Wow, modern medicine. I guess I'm not ready to join Rebecca yet. Sit down, please."

Cassy took a deep breath, relieved that he still had his sense of humor. "Okay, but I'm only allowed to stay a few minutes."

Ben turned to face her. "I need to tell you something before—" He took a deep breath. "Rebecca and I never had children."

"I remember you mentioned that."

"She took a special interest in you when you were in high school."

Cassy looked down. "I really didn't deserve it."

"My senior year in high school, she was a freshman. I had my eye on her. She had green eyes like you do. A few years later I was attending U.C. Berkeley when I heard she was pregnant, unmarried, and had to drop out of school."

"You don't have to tell me this. Maybe you should rest."

He hesitated a moment and went on. "Rebecca had a baby girl when she was seventeen. The father, Mike, joined the army, and the baby was adopted. She desperately wanted to make visits, but everyone told her to make a clean break. That it would be best for the child. It was the times."

Cassy fidgeted in the stiff hospital chair. She felt uncomfortable hearing such personal information. Still, she wanted to be polite. "What ever happened to the father?"

"He was one of the first Americans in North Africa, and something of a hero. He died taking out one of Rommel's tanks."

"Did Rebecca know?"

"Nobody told her at the time. She read it in the papers. She got her high school diploma at home and enrolled at San Francisco State. I saw her again at spring break."

"And you fell in love?"

"Well, I did. Some guys avoided her like she had leprosy. Like I say, she had this…reputation. Other guys figured she was loose and wanted to go out with her. She could spot those guys and stayed away. After a while, she trusted me and even liked me. She told me all about her past, and I told her, 'It's water over the dam.' Didn't mean a hill of beans to me. Hell, I was no boy scout. I asked her to marry me, but she said she had to be sure. She didn't want to make another mistake."

Cassy struggled to maintain her composure. She knew Ben needed to rest, but he seemed intent on finishing his story. "What made her say yes?"

His voice grew stronger. "I signed with the National Guard in '41 and got sent to Camp Claiborne in Louisiana. When Pearl Harbor got bombed, the army extended my tour of active duty to the duration of the war plus six months. I went home for Christmas, where I was something of a celebrity. We were married a week before my regiment shipped out. In the beginning, it was a great adventure. I even got a this." He raised the sleeve on his gown, exposing a tattoo.

"Is that a red bull?"

"Yeah. That's what they called the 34th division. In '44, I learned that my brother, Syd, had died in combat in Sicily. I started counting the days until the war ended."

"It must have been dreadful. Did your wife ever see her daughter?"

"No, but I did. Didn't know it at the time. After the war, I finished my engineering degree at Berkeley on the G.I. bill. In the sixties I worked for the Highway Department. We had steady work because of Ike's Interstate Project. Hell, it was bigger than going to the moon. I was in charge of a project that would go through San Francisco to the Golden Gate. Couldn't believe the hostility it created. At one planning meeting, a woman ripped us up one side and down the other. Said we were pushing poor people out of their homes and destroying the city. The project got killed. I thought she was a kook and had someone check her out."

"Mom told me stories about scuttling that freeway. Maybe they knew each other."

He hesitated before going on. "The woman at the meeting…her name…Sandy O'Neal."

Cassy gasped. "That's my mother's name!"

Ben turned away. His voice trembled. "Before Rebecca passed away, she wanted me to know more details about her daughter. The adopting family, the O'Neals, named her Sandra…your mom…my wife was your grandmother."

12 Trouble

The weekend agility trial finished Sunday at dusk, and Liam loaded the van. Storm saw her first in the dim light. His wagging tail pounded a staccato rhythm on the metal door. Cassy hurried over. He'd been puzzled when she vanished the previous day without a word, so he was glad to see her again, even though she looked distraught.

"Oh, Liam, I'm so glad you're still here."

"Is something wrong?"

"That nice old man I told you about yesterday had a heart attack."

"Geez. Is he okay?"

Cassy took a deep breath. "We won't know for a few days. I just got back from the hospital."

"What happened?"

"At the house last night. He got all worked up. I called an ambulance right away." She began weeping. "I'm such a screw up."

He hesitated, then put his arms around her. "I'm sure it wasn't your fault." He held her tight, and her sobbing accelerated. "What happened?"

Cassy wiped her eyes with the back of her hand. "An old boy friend showed up and made an awful scene. I thought I saw his truck here yesterday and freaked."

"Is that why you left? Is he stalking you?"

"I don't know. I can't get it together. Just when it looks like everything's under control, it falls apart. I've got no job, no money, and then I find out I'm someone's granddaughter, or his wife's granddaughter, or...I don't know what's going on."

"Hold on. Are you talking about the man who had the heart attack? You didn't know they were your grandparents?"

"I don't know. Just his wife. It's all happening so fast."

Liam's instincts told him he shouldn't get mixed up with confused women, but pretty girls have a way of overcoming that uncertainty. "Will you be all right?"

"I'm afraid this guy might come back," she said. "Myst is alone."

"I could follow you home."

She touched his arm. "I'd be so grateful. I know it's a lot to ask, but could you stay the night?"

Liam's head was spinning. He hesitated a moment. "Sure. Is there a sofa?"

"You could stay in Ben's room."

"That wouldn't feel right. The sofa will be fine."

At the house, Cassy found Liam a blanket and pillow. He slept fitfully in the living room with Storm on the floor nearby. At six o'clock Monday morning, Liam told Cassy he'd come back later that day. He dropped Storm off at his house and taught classes all day. He suffered through the after-school faculty meeting, and by the time he picked up Storm and headed back to Sebastopol, it was dark. He noticed a broken rear taillight on the passenger side of his van, which must have happened that day in the school parking lot. Smelling something pungent inside, like burnt rope, he checked to make sure the emergency brake had been released.

"Storm, what have you been into today?" he said, half-heartedly accusing the dog.

As he drove, he pondered the vaguely familiar odor. A rotating red light in his rear view mirror and an ear-piercing siren shocked him to attention. A quick glance at his speedometer showed he was 5 MPH over the speed limit.

He pulled to the side of the road and waited for what seemed an eternity. The blinding glare of the highway patrol car's spotlight reflected from the rear view mirror into his eyes. What could be taking so long for a routine traffic stop? Then he remembered the smell, and the boys he'd caught smoking in the restroom at a school dance. His heart pounded. The policeman approached slowly and beamed his flashlight into Liam's face.

Trying to control his nerves, he smiled into the light. "What's the problem, officer?"

"Are you aware your right rear taillight is broken? The light's out."

Liam, somewhat relieved that it wasn't something more serious, said, "No. It must have happened in the school parking lot. I teach chemistry at the high school."

"Let me see your driver's license."

While Liam fumbled with his wallet, the policeman turned his flashlight on the floor of the van where the green depths of Storm's eyes reflected back. The cop sniffed a couple times. "Would you open your ashtray?"

"My ashtray?" Liam numbly complied and exposed what he recognized from his duty checking restrooms. There it was, like dog crap on his shoe: a smoked roach butt with a clip attached. "Look, this isn't mine. I don't even smoke."

"Are you aware your driver's license can be suspended for six months for possession of a controlled substance?"

"I don't know the law because I've never had reason to, in the past, or now. That's not mine. Why did you stop me tonight?"

"In addition to the broken taillight, we got an anonymous telephone call tipping us off about your van. Let me see your vehicle registration."

As Liam opened the glove compartment, the beam of light from the policeman's flashlight reflected off a small cellophane packet containing what looked like dirty brown rock salt. A glass cylinder with a bulb on one end lay on top.

"Hand me the bag and the glass pipe," the voice behind the flashlight ordered.

"This isn't mine. Someone else put that stuff here." Liam handed it over. His face burned, his mouth was dry.

"Did you say you were a chemistry teacher? I'd say you've got a bag of crystal meth. The color means homemade. You've got a smoked joint, a roach clip, a bong, and a bag of crank. Get out of the car. You're under arrest for illegal possession of controlled substances and drug paraphernalia. Put your hands behind your back. You have the right to remain silent—"

"Somebody planted this. This is a mistake."

"We'll let the judge decide that. I'll have animal control get the dog. The van will be impounded and searched."

The officer handcuffed Liam and led him to the patrol car.

13 Not Five Stars

Liam figured he'd hit rock bottom when the jail deputy ordered, "Take your clothes off." When he heard, "Bend over," he no longer had any doubt.

"Spread 'em." The deputy seemed to enjoy administering the humiliating search. "He's clean, book him."

The supervisor set the standard bail for his arrest at $8,000. An officer took his fingerprints and a photo. He said, "We'll have an orange jump suit for you in the morning."

The deputy led Liam to an overnight holding cell. A metal door opened into a concrete room fifteen by twenty feet with wooden benches. Although a sign stipulated an eight-person capacity, eighteen inmates were crowded in smelly proximity, most of them sitting on the floor. A metal toilet with no seat or toilet paper was located in a corner. There were no windows. A single light bulb remained on all night, and the primary activity of the inmates consisted of sitting and staring.

Liam was distraught. His fingerprints were on the drug paraphernalia because he'd handed them to the cop. He might need a public defender. And he was worried about Storm. Where had they taken the dog? He needed to call someone and get Storm released.

A young man approached. "Hey, cuz. The man forgot to turn the heat on. How'd you like to give a bro your jacket?"

Could things get any worse? Liam was into his second sleepless night, charged with a felony, and some thug in the holding tank wanted to rip off his jacket. "Sorry, bro. Can't do that."

The young cellmate took a step closer. "I guess I didn't make it clear enough. Give me your jacket so I won't have to mess up your sorry-looking ugly face."

A bored-looking man wearing a gray, hooded sweatshirt mumbled, "You tell 'im, Lamar."

Liam normally would do anything possible to avoid a conflict, but he'd reached his limit. He stood up from the floor and stepped toward his antagonist. "I apologize. I guess I didn't make myself clear. You can't have my jacket, but if you'd like your teeth rearranged, then make my day." He couldn't believe he'd said that.

The man in the hoody laughed. "Hey, Lamar, I think you're up against Dirty Harry."

The amused spectators, those who weren't passed out drunk, burst into laughter. Lamar suddenly relaxed and held out his hand. "Hey, cuz, no hard feelings. Let's shake."

Liam cautiously shook hands. "Hey, man, we're good."

The jailer, who had probably been answering nature's call, reappeared. He raised his billy club and gave it a few half-hearted shakes. "Listen, girls. Hold it down. Don't make me come in there and put you to sleep."

Hoody replied, "Yasssir, Boss. I'se awful thirsty. Could you bring us a nice cold beer?"

The jailer sneered. "Listen, funny man, that's the worst plantation dialect I've ever heard. Now shut up."

Liam took this opportunity to make a request of his own. "Can I make a phone call?"

"In the morning. We're busy right now."

The jailer sat down near the cell, put his feet up on a nearby chair, folded his arms, and closed his eyes.

Hoody sat on the floor next to Liam. "This your first time? Not exactly five stars, is it?"

Liam, a little apprehensive, said, "First time. Someone planted drugs in my van. Set me up. How about you?"

"DUI. Failed the street tests. Tried to tell the man in blue I had dizzy spells. Something I picked up in Nam. Can't get a job. A lot of people have bad vibes about vets."

"That's tough. What kind of job are you looking for?"

"Handyman. Metal work. Make furniture or just about anything. Here, have my business card. The deputy missed it when I got searched. If you hear of something, I'd appreciate a call. That's my name, Tom Jackson."

Liam couldn't put his finger on it, but there was something he liked about Tom Jackson. He sympathized with a veteran who didn't get a warm welcome home. "You know, I have friends looking for someone who can make dog sport equipment. I'll pass on your name."

He proceeded to explain agility equipment to Tom, who listened intently and offered several useful suggestions. They chatted for the next hour. Exhausted, Liam finally fell asleep on the concrete floor for a few hours.

In the morning, Liam debated whom to call. His principal? Too humiliating. He didn't know Cassy's telephone number. As much as he dreaded it, his best chance for help would probably be his ex-wife, Myra.

After the most miserable night of his life, breakfast for the inmates consisted of bologna and cheese sandwiches referred to as "Johnnies," an oatmeal cookie, and coffee as thick as maple syrup. An hour later, he called Myra.

At 11 a.m., the day jailer unlocked the cell. "Gallagher. Let's go. You've made bail."

The desk sergeant handed Liam an envelope containing his personal items. "Sign here. It's all there, except for the dope, of course."

Liam squinted as he exited the building into bright sunlight. He spotted Myra waiting for him. She must have been showing houses that morning and looked smart in her tailored gray suit. Why did she look happy to see him? He rubbed his two-day stubble. "Hi. I'm sorry I look like such a mess."

"I'd say Indiana Jones or maybe Lawrence of Arabia too long in the desert. Missed you this month. We need to stay in touch."

"I really appreciate your help."

Her low-heeled, black Italian shoes clicked noisily on the sidewalk as they moved briskly toward her Buick. She had recently turned forty and was still quite attractive. She wore more makeup than Liam liked, but her frenetic real estate activity kept her trim and fit. Her skirt slid up over her knees as she climbed into the car. "Where to?" she asked.

Liam debated with himself. Which smelled worse, the drunk tank or the stale smoke odor in her car? "Let's get the van first," he said.

"You know, I believe your story. We lived together for twelve years."

"Thanks."

"If you really want to thank me, then talk to me in something other than monosyllables."

"Please, don't start."

Myra took a long breath. She clutched the steering wheel tighter with her left hand, fumbled in her Gucci handbag with her right, and found a Virginia Slims 10-pack. She glanced at Liam, who mechanically pushed in the car lighter. After a moment, she extracted the lighter, lit up, took a deep drag, and exhaled. "I hear you have a dog."

Liam hit a power switch opening his window an inch. "Yeah, his name is Storm. I have to retrieve him from the pound."

Myra opened her window an inch. "I know you hate cigarette smoke. I laughed out loud when I heard you were arrested for dope. I mean, I can't conjure up that image. Why would someone set you up?"

"I think this guy saw me talking to his former girlfriend. He grew weed in Northern California."

She took a second drag on her SuperSlim100 and extinguished it. "So you've met someone. Good for you."

"Nothing serious. We're just friends."

"If I know you, you're serious. Who knows about the girl?"

Liam squirmed in his seat and stared out the window. "How's the real estate market?"

She reached for another cigarette and pushed in the car lighter herself. "You're supposed to ask if I'm seeing anyone." She lit up and took two quick puffs. "The market is actually going through the roof. I have three deals in escrow, and I'll close another this weekend. I could do more, but ten-hour days, six days a week are my limit. One thing about real estate, it's the safest investment you can make, and I've got rentals that always need work."

"Could you use a handyman to fix up the rentals?"

"Why? Are you looking to earn a little weekend cash?"

"Hardly, but I know a guy I'd recommend." He reached into his pocket.

"You're just full of surprises these days."

He handed her Tom Jackson's card. "So are you seeing anyone?"

"No one special. That Reno thing was a big mistake. I already told you I screwed up. I'm too busy to get involved right now."

"I like your new car."

"Oh God, I drive a Buick because that's what real estate people do."

"You can't go wrong with a GM car."

"To tell the truth, I'd like a Land Rover."

"Then get one."

She looked amused. "For some strange reason, I like you more now that you've been arrested. Kind of exciting."

"If you want excitement, get an SUV."

Myra inhaled deeply and blew smoke out the partially open window. "You never got it. People need a real life and a fantasy life."

"You never told me about a fantasy life."

"Well, you don't talk about it. But most people need to break out now and then."

"This girl I met lived in a tree for a month."

Myra glanced at Liam in disbelief. "Oh, that's better. Are you serious?"

"Yes, she protested cutting down redwood trees."

"How wonderful. I like her already. She lived in a tree and has a boyfriend who grows pot."

"A former boy friend."

"There's hope for you, after all. If you get tired of playing Tarzan and Jane, we should get together. We can still be friends."

Liam decided to change the subject. "I had a bologna sandwich for breakfast."

"Aren't you the lucky one? Tell you what—let's get lunch. There's this nice place on River Road. I've closed a few deals there."

"I appreciate your help, but I'm not fit for polite company right now. Could we get my van so I can pick up Storm? I'd like to go home and clean up. Maybe we can have dinner sometime."

"How about tomorrow?"

"Let me get back to you. I'm messed up right now."

Myra extinguished her half-smoked cigarette. "I'll call you tonight."

Liam closed his eyes. "Okay."

She fumbled in her purse for another cigarette. "Damn, empty. We'll have to make a quick stop. You don't mind, do you?"

14 When the Dawn Comes

By Tuesday night, Liam was suddenly the best-known man in Sonoma County. The local newspaper produced brisk sales with its headline story, "Local Teacher Going to Pot," the teacher's photo captured from the latest edition of the Sonoma Central High yearbook.

Shortly before four o'clock Liam had retrieved his van, rescued Storm, and returned home. One of the earliest messages in a full answering machine came from a reporter wanting another angle on his hottest story. He pleaded for an interview to hear Liam's side. He wanted a picture of the accused next to his van. Liam guessed that resurrected images of the sixties would produce an interesting slant. He clenched his teeth and saluted the answering machine with his middle finger.

One nervous-sounding message came from Malcolm Honeycutt, his principal, who assured Liam that he was standing behind him, although he needed to suspend him for the rest of the school year until all the facts were revealed. He asked his disgraced teacher to see him that evening at six o'clock, after the campus had cleared out.

After a night in the slammer, Liam desperately needed a nap, but after an equally necessary shower and shave, he watched the lead story on the five o'clock news instead. A taped on-the-scene report from Sonoma Central High showed that the teachers stood behind him. Mr. Posada, the History teacher, explained that the reported events were out of character for Mr. Gallagher. "There must be a perfectly logical explanation." Student Richie Boynton, wearing his baseball cap backwards, considered the accused a really cool dude. A small group of parents gathered at the entrance of the high school and demanded that education be purged of bad teachers. Mrs. Carney screamed into the television camera, "I'm tired as hell seeing my tax money wasted on a school that can't solve its drug problem. This whole mess is a disgrace! I'm going to enroll my daughter in a private school."

This lead story was followed by updates of recent Bay Area rapes and murders. When Channel 6 cut to the pizza commercial, Liam hit the power button on the TV and popped his frozen dinner into the microwave.

Liam pulled into the Central High School parking lot promptly at six and parked next to the space reserved for Malcolm Honeycutt's late model BMW. He moved quickly down the hallway to Malcolm's domain. One of Malcolm's first projects as new principal was to reorganize the administrative suite. Two smaller offices had a common wall removed. A large glass window was installed on the south wall so Malcolm could enjoy a pleasant view of the nearby woods. Liam's noisy footsteps on the tiled hallway were muffled as soon as he entered the plush carpeted office with freshly painted walls.

Malcolm Honeycutt, a small man with a neatly trimmed beard and mustache, looked up from his perfectly ordered oak desk, forced a smile, and greeted his one-time teacher of the year. "Come in, Liam. Close the door, please, and have a seat."

As far as Liam knew, there was no one else in the school except the night crew. He guessed Malcolm wanted no witnesses. The elbow protectors on Malcolm's tweed sport coat seemed consistent with his desired image as academic leader of the school, but the perfect knot in his tie appeared to be choking him. His eyes bulged as if he had an overactive thyroid. If Central hadn't been a smoke-free school, Liam guessed Malcolm would have been smoking a pipe.

"I want you to know we're all behind you, one hundred percent."

"Thanks, it has been a little rough lately."

"Is there anything I can do for you?"

"Well, if you have a cot, I could use some sleep."

Malcolm forced a weak smile, picked up a pen, and tapped it twice before he spoke again. "I think you can imagine how this whole incident has affected the school. It's been a zoo around here. Numerous phone calls from parents, as well as the president of the school board. I explained what a fine teacher you've been all these years. The truth is, this has been a public relations nightmare. We all know you're innocent until proven guilty, but I hope you understand why I had to suspend you."

"I know you're just doing your job. I want to get this over with and get back to teaching."

Malcolm's lower lip quivered slightly. "Right. I'm sure it will all work out. It's just that...you know how the public is going to see this. Where's there's smoke, there's fire."

Liam took a deep breath, trying to control the anger welling inside. "I can assure you, there's no fire."

"Right. It's just that Central needs to maintain its image. You know, of course, we have our application in as a State Distinguished School. It's important we keep the good will of our parents."

"What are you getting at?"

"I had a chance to talk with the district attorney today. He thinks the felony charges are pretty weak. If you plead guilty to the possession charge, that will only be a misdemeanor. You could continue teaching."

Liam's heart raced. He'd reached a breaking point—a pending divorce, a false arrest, a night in jail—and now this. "I'm not pleading guilty for something I didn't do. How can you even suggest such a thing?"

"Look, I know I can't force your decision, but I think it would be in the best interest of our school, and yourself, to put this behind us as soon as possible. You might consider transferring to another school. Get a fresh start. I can write you a recommendation. It'll be better for everyone."

"Don't you think that's like sweeping dirt under the carpet?"

"Don't take it the wrong way. It's just that it would make everything easier."

"It would make your job easier, wouldn't it? Fewer phone calls from parents."

"I'm only thinking about what's best for our students."

Aggressive anger was new to Liam. He struggled to suppress it. "You want to do the right thing?"

"Right, that's the spirit. We've always been a team at Central High."

"A team? Well, I agree, and I'm not going to quit on my students, the other teachers, or myself. I'm innocent, and I'm going to prove it. You can take your transfer and stick it."

Malcolm's sickly smile disappeared. "That's not professional."

"Maybe not, but maybe the other teachers will be interested in what your one hundred percent support looks like." Liam got up and moved toward the door.

Malcolm raised both hands, feigning surrender. "You misunderstood…please sit down. Look at this from my point of view."

"No, you've done that for both of us. I'm outta here."

Cassy waited alone in Sebastopol, unaware of Liam's arrest. Occasionally, she'd glance out the front window, looking for him. When he left early Monday morning, he'd promised to return that afternoon. She nervously surveyed the street, hoping not to see Frank's truck. She believed he was stalking her.

Myst seemed to sense Cassy's anxiety and followed her around the house, never more than a few steps away. The border collie slept fitfully, alertly raising her head at any unfamiliar sound.

Around midnight, Cassy woke from a fitful sleep. She rose and looked out the bedroom window. The full moon reminded her of time spent nestled in the branches of a redwood tree. The forest had been shrouded in fog most nights, but on a rare clear night the moon gave her comfort, while the tall trees moaned in the coastal wind.

Later, Cassy woke again. The moon hovered low in the northwest, and the streetlights cast a dull glow on the darkened neighborhood. The streetlights died. A new day had begun.

On Tuesday, Cassy visited Ben at the hospital. After dinner, the streetlights, initially dim, returned to full strength, and the shadows grew darker, sharper, and more ominous. Withered leaves and dust blew sporadically across the ground. The harvest moon reappeared low in the northeast, surprisingly large, and very orange.

Myst rose to her feet, alert. Cassy moved the window curtain, peered outside, and saw a van parking in front of the house. The driver opened the side door. She recognized the large black dog that bolted out.

15 Strong Medicine

Ben had been home from the hospital for several days. He looked up alertly when he heard a car door shut, and then felt relief, perhaps because the visitor had arrived in a van rather than the pickup truck driven by Cassy's old boyfriend. Reluctantly, he answered the door.

"Hello. I'm a friend of Cassy's…and her dog, Myst. I mean, your dog, Myst. Would she happen to be in?"

He scrutinized the stranger. "You look familiar."

Liam hesitated. "I think we met in the park awhile back. Well, we didn't really meet, but we spoke to each other. I was just passing through, and you were sitting there feeding the squirrels."

Ben leaned on his cane and stared at the tall, lean stranger. Cassy certainly had questionable taste when it came to picking her friends. First, there was that scoundrel who caused him to have the heart attack, and now this tongue-tied loser.

"You're the guy with the squirrel-chasing Lab."

Liam looked down at his feet. "I'm really sorry about that. My dog should have been on a leash."

"You've got to learn to control that dog. He's a menace."

"Maybe I should come back another time."

"It's not usually the dog's fault, you know."

Liam took a step backward. "Would you tell Cassy I was here?"

Ben stroked the stubble on his chin. "Didn't mean to sound like such a grouch. The last visitor was a real SOB." The corners of his mouth turned slightly upward, and he looked past Liam at nothing in particular. "I had a Lab when I was a boy. Did he ever like the water! He could smell it a mile away. I remember…you called your dog Storm. That's a strange name."

"That's right. He's a flat-coated retriever, a rescue from Hurricane Andrew."

"My dog acted just like your Lab, but I trained him. Smartest dog I've ever seen. You've got to train your dog, or he's going to get himself and you into a lot of trouble."

"Well, I'm working on it. It's hard to find time—"

"Heavens to Betsy, man, make time. That's no excuse. My dog Myst is trained. Smart as the Lab I told you about. Cassy's out walking her right now. I've been laid up awhile, or I'd walk the dog."

"She told me about your hospital stay. I'm glad to see you're home."

"Hell, if they'd kept me at that miserable place another day, I'd have one foot in the wastebasket. As soon as I got home, I felt better. Haven't felt this good in years!" He raised his cane and waved it in cadence with his booming voice. "I'm taking blue pills for the ticker. Had white ones in the hospital, Comb-a-tin or something like that."

Liam relaxed. "I've heard having a pet can be therapeutic."

"Hell, you've got that right. Come inside and sit a spell. She mentioned you. She should be back any minute. How about a beer?"

"I don't want to impose. I'll come back later."

"Great Scott! Will you stop that?"

"Okay. I'll have what you're having."

Ben opened the door, grabbed Liam's arm, and pulled him inside. "Sit there," he said and pointed to a chair. When he returned from the kitchen with two bottles of lite beer, Liam was gazing at the portrait over the fireplace. "That's my wife, Rebecca. She was Cassy's grandmother."

"I can see the resemblance."

"She passed on a few years ago."

"I'm sorry. You must miss her a lot."

"Yeah." His voiced trailed off, and he burped. "In case you're wondering, I'm allowed a beer now and then. The hospital guy insisted I have someone come in five times a week to clean and cook and whatever. That would be Ida. I think she's originally from Guatemala. Once I'm back to normal, I'll start fixing this place up. The fence could use a fresh coat of paint." He took a swig from his beer bottle. "Cassy told me you were a teacher."

"I'm trying to work out some problems right now."

"I heard. My God, how can you stand it? I mean the kids today. Baggy pants, drugs, all that violence."

"Well, it's not always easy, but most students are doing the best they can. The good kids don't make the news."

Ben shook his finger. "Everything comes too easy. When I was their age, I was in North Africa and Italy with a lot of other kids, taking Nazi fire. Trying to stay alive."

"It must have been rough."

"We got yellow pills in Africa...to prevent malaria. Man, were they bitter. Guys had headaches and threw up. A few went nuts. The doctors didn't know if it was the pills or the war."

"The pills may have been Atabrine. The Japanese cut off the supply of quinine."

"Yeah, I knew that. The pills backfired in more ways than one. They caused diarrhea. A lot of guys quit taking them."

"I suppose they weren't needed in Italy."

"One day in Italy we made a big fuss over a beautiful white dog that wandered into camp. For a few moments, we felt human again. A major came by and shot the dog. Of course, we were pissed off. He told us German snipers trained large white dogs to hang around enemy troops because it helped spot us. Soldiers are trained not to give a second thought to killing other soldiers, but shooting a dog...that was rough."

"We owe a lot to your generation." Liam glanced out the window at the back yard. "Tell you what. Would you let me paint your fence?"

"Are you serious? What do you charge?"

"Nothing. Or maybe you'd let Cassy and I can set up some dog agility equipment on your lawn and practice?"

Ben stuck out his hand. "Deal."

Liam painted the fence and relished his new role as handyman for the next two weeks. It gave him an excuse to see Cassy, as well. Whenever possible, they worked together to build rudimentary agility equipment in the mornings, and practiced with the dogs in the afternoons. No one noticed the dark Ford pickup cruising by late at night, sometimes parking a block away. The longhaired driver quietly watched the house with the freshly painted picket fence.

November days grew shorter, the evenings cooler. The usual seasonal drought concluded, and the rainy season began in earnest. Coastal hills and fields came alive and quickly turned green. The gentle rain would soon be replaced by winter storms bringing heavy winds and flooding. Sonoma County has been widely recognized as a good place to sell umbrellas.

Cassy earned money as a house and pet sitter. She had five clients at twenty dollars a day. She even found time to begin an evening class at Sonoma State. Working alone with Myst, Cassy pointed and called out the names of equipment while standing still. Myst quickly learned the names of all the obstacles. Cassy could take one step, turn her shoulders, change arms, and direct her dog around the courses.

Ben made rapid progress, and his doctor changed the blue pills to green. He enjoyed watching Myst and Storm in their training sessions. Every now and then, he'd offer suggestions.

"Liam, you were a little late with that call. Hell, the dog was already off course in the tunnel before you called him to the jump. Watch the way Cassy handled that sequence, you'll eventually catch on."

Liam grimaced, but thanked him for his helpfulness.

The two handlers made plans to enter their pets in the Bay Barkers event over Thanksgiving weekend at Cal State Hayward. That would be the first trial for Myst.

Liam finally got some good news at his arraignment. Felony charges were dropped. Myra's bail payment was returned. However, misdemeanor possession charges required him to appear in court again the following month.

One evening, as Liam parked in front of Ben's house, a dark black pickup pulled in behind him. The longhaired driver jumped out and confronted Liam, his face so close there was no missing the bloodshot eyes and a pungent smell radiating from his breath and clothing. He shouted in Liam's face.

"You're a fucking loser, man!"

"Who in the hell are you?" Liam replied. But he knew. This was the slime-ball stalking Cassy.

Frank did his best imitation of a puffer fish trying to appear bigger than he really was. "Keep away from my girlfriend, butthead."

A patrol car pulled up at the same time Cassy came running from the house. "Let the police handle this," she called. "I phoned them five minutes ago when I saw Frank's truck circling the block."

Liam recognized the patrolman as the cop who had pulled him over two weeks before.

"Officer, this guy reeks of marijuana. If you search his truck, you'll find the evidence. This is the guy who framed me."

Frank quickly backed away from Liam. "This piece of crap is a dealer. I told him to stay away from my girlfriend."

Cassy looked at him in disgust. "I'm not your girlfriend. Officer, that truck is dirty."

The officer looked puzzled. Domestic confrontations can turn dangerous. He moved toward Frank. "I'd like you to empty your pockets, please."

Frank regained his composure, sneered and replied, "Unless you're looking to be sued, I do not consent to a search of my person, belongings, or vehicle. I retain my fourth amendment rights and all other rights under the United States Constitution and will say nothing unless an attorney is present."

Liam rolled his eyes. "That's hardly the spontaneous statement of someone who has nothing to hide."

The policeman pursed his lips and shook his head. "I agree, but he's right. Under the law, I need something more in order to search him."

Liam grimaced. "How was searching my van any different?"

"Because I stopped you for a violation…a broken tail-light. That gave me the right to investigate further." The policeman turned to Frank. "Look, if I see you in this neighborhood again, I'm going to detain you as a public nuisance. Am I clear?"

"Crystal." Frank made no attempt to hide the smirk spreading across his face. "Am I under arrest? If not, I really need to get going. Have a nice day." He got into his truck, started the engine and drove slowly down the street into the darkness. The faint sound of his laughter drifted on the breeze.

16 Velcro Dog

The Bay Barkers' Agility Trial
Cal Sate Hayward, Meiklejohn Lawn

Next in the ring was a basset hound, so low to the ground that, as the dog ran, his belly occasionally bounced on the grass. Dog and handler profiles matched, and spectators hoped CPR would not be required at the conclusion of this entry. As the man and his basset waddled toward the teeter-totter, the guy's pants fell down around his ankles. He kept going, trying to pull his pants up. The dog tipped the teeter and stopped in the yellow zone. Realizing his handler wasn't with him, he turned around and went back up the teeter in the wrong direction. The handler bent over, duck-walked forward still trying to pull up his pants, but didn't watch where he was going. When the teeter tipped downward, it smacked the handler on the top of his head, laying him flat on his back. The basset kept coming and sat down on the end of the teeter, trapping the handler, who flopped around like a fish out of water. Finally, he gave up and lay there, quivering.

While the judge lifted the teeter, the dog maintained a classic sit position. The handler struggled to get up. He forgot that his pants were still around his ankles and promptly went down again. When he tried to get up the second time, he was laughing so hard he couldn't stand. The third time was the charm, and the spectators gave him a hearty Bronx cheer.

This was Liam's first competition in a new venue called NADAC, the North American Dog Agility Council, and the first trial ever for Cassy and Myst. Unlike the twisty-turny courses on which he and Storm had competed before, these were wide open and flowing. Furthermore, mixed breeds were welcome. The opening and closing sequences had three jumps in a straight line. The central part of the course consisted of gentle arcing challenges. There was no pause table to interrupt the dog's velocity. The larger dogs welcomed the opportunity to stretch their legs and run close to top speed. If the dogs were cars, this would be Formula One racing. The casual observer might conclude these courses were too easy, but there were subtle challenges. Because the dogs ran much faster, an ill-timed command by a handler made off-courses more likely. The dogs' speed made pausing in the yellow zones on the contact obstacles an iffy challenge.

Liam recognized many of the same competitors he'd seen at past trials, including Preston Wadsworth and his magnificent Australian shepherd, Ringo. When Preston wasn't judging, his dog won many of these events. Liam recalled the time Preston as judge had whistled Storm off the course.

Cassy shifted her weight nervously from one foot to the other. Myst rolled onto her back and wiggled from side to side as if to relieve a phantom itch.

The gate steward alerted the competitors, whose dogs were arranged in alphabetical order. "Lucy in the ring, Merlin on deck, Myst in the hole…" A minute later, "Merlin in the ring, Myst on deck…"

As Merlin began running, Cassy and Myst moved into a narrow chute to be in position to enter the ring. Cassy closed her eyes and mentally reviewed the course. Myst nervously chewed on grass.

The gate steward called out, "Myst in the ring…"

As they moved to the starting line, the dog tucked her tail and looked anxiously from side to side. Because the opening sequence promised to be fast, Cassy walked forward to jump number two and started running.

"Come."

Myst lowered her ears and trotted to the first jump. Cassy slowed to a walk, her dog a few feet from her side. They finished the course with no mistakes, but were more than ten seconds over the standard course time.

Cassy leashed her dog and walked over to Liam, her shoulders slumped. "Well, that sucked! I thought all border collies were sheepdog fast. She looked scared to death. You'd think we were attached by Velcro."

He thought a moment. "She ran soft the first few times we worked out. Maybe she'll get faster when she gains confidence. If you like, we can skip the events tomorrow."

"I'm not quitting. Don't even suggest it."

The message was loud and clear. Liam made a fist and Cassy smacked it with her own.

As the day progressed her dog did get faster, especially on the finishing sequences, perhaps sensing the opportunity to get out of the ring. But she was still slow and never more than a few feet from Cassy, who could protect her from imaginary demons.

By late Sunday afternoon many competitors, including Preston Wadsworth and the other accomplished handlers, were done for the day and had left the trial. Liam joined a handful of spectators to watch the last event for Novice dogs only.

Most of the Novice dogs looked worn out after two days of trialing. It was more the mental strain than the physical effort of eight runs. Kenneled outside, surrounded by constant activity and barking dogs, the unfamiliar setting took its toll. Surprisingly, Myst looked more intense than at any other time during the weekend.

Liam watched Myst quiver in anticipation as she waited for the hand signal to begin. The dog bolted from the start line, quickly opening a gap of fifty feet from her dumbfounded handler. Cassy stopped, turned her shoulders to the right and drew the required path with her left hand, as if she were holding an imaginary crayon. Her dog turned immediately. Myst focused on Cassy's shoulders and turned to the right. She blasted through a tunnel and focused on the jump ahead. She seemed to listen intently for Cassy's commands.

"Out."

Myst moved quickly away and around the jump, entering another tunnel. She instinctively knew how to work at a great distance. She followed Cassy's body language and turned sharply left to the A-Frame.

"Scramble."

Myst raced up and down the A-Frame. She froze at the bottom, two front feet in the dirt and two hind feet in the yellow zone. The crowd oohed in admiration. Then she was off and running again.

"Teeter."

Myst hesitated when the teeter touched the ground. Cassy turned her right shoulder sharply toward her dog.

"Weave."

The plastic poles bounced off the sides of Myst's body, first on the left and then on the right. She accelerated out of the last weave pole on the left side and looked to Cassy for direction.

"Here."

Myst turned sharply inward, went up, across, and down the dog walk. She again froze with her hind feet in the yellow zone of the dog walk. The tire was next. She looked toward the far end of the ring for directions.

"Jump. Go On."

She streaked for the finish. Centuries of instinctive behavior bred into the sheepdog controlled her. She had a job to do. She raced toward the finish at full speed, skimming the last three jumps.

Liam watched in amazement. What the hell was that? Where did that come from? Cassy, by switching arms and drawing the correct path with her imaginary crayon had controlled Myst's movements. She barely moved more than ten feet during the run.

The onlookers were shouting. Cassy was jumping up and down and squealing.

After leaving the ring, Cassy explained. "Some days when we trained alone, I'd be tired, so I'd just stand in one spot and direct her from a distance. I loved the thought that she was running free, but we still felt connected. The people this weekend ran their dogs as if they were doing obedience, keeping them close, always in complete control. I was afraid they'd think I was lazy unless I ran like they did, but this last time Myst got so far ahead, there was no way I could keep up. So I just stood there like a traffic cop."

Liam smiled. "You know…border collies are sheepdogs. They're able to move completely out of sight when herding. Maybe you've got something. Most everyone treats their dogs like they're attached by Velcro. Let's work on this distance handling. Myst seems more at ease when handled that way."

17 Madera

Cold tule fog covered California's central valley in December.
Because visibility was no more than thirty yards, Liam followed another vehicle at 20 MPH on highway 152. He leaned
forward in the driver's seat, bug-eyed, grasping the steering
wheel in a death grip. After two hours they approached Los
Banos, still an hour from Madera.

Cassy woke and straightened in her seat. "Has it been
foggy long?"

"Only the last couple hours."

"I'm hungry." She opened a cooler and removed two
bottles of orange juice.

Liam reached out with his right hand until he felt a white
powdered doughnut being passed in the darkness, which he
wolfed in one gulp. He resumed his two-handed strangula-
tion of the steering wheel, looking as if he had a severe case
of the mumps.

Cassy had arranged for Ida to spend the weekend with
Ben. He insisted it wasn't necessary, but she managed to
change his mind.

This was their second trial together and their first trip
into the valley. Slowed by fog, the normal two-hour commute

took more than three hours. Liam desperately needed a rest stop when they pulled into the Madera County Fairgrounds at 7:45 a.m. Mindful that a good parking spot was desirable, Liam dropped Cassy off at the restrooms and continued on to the show area. He spread out a mat near the ring to claim territory and limped toward the restroom. He saw her emerging from the cold mist.

"The restrooms are locked," she grumbled.

While Cassy tended to the dogs, Liam started to set up a canopy. He was startled by an unfamiliar, but cheery female voice.

"I'm surry dear, but you can't set up there."

"Pardon me?" Liam turned and saw a strapping figure looming over him. She had a pleasant round face with rosy cheeks. Her braided blond hair was barely visible through a stocking cap pulled tightly over her ears. Black rubber boots reached halfway to her knees.

"We're trying to keep the area eboot here clear for the food vendor coming later today. Perheps you could set up oot there." She pointed to an area on the other side of the ring barely visible in the fog. "I'm Olga Svenson. Let me know if I can help oot."

"Is it possible someone could unlock the restrooms?"

"Oh, you puur man. I have the key. I'll hurry over right noo."

Liam thanked her and soon took care of his number one priority. Next, he hauled the mat, canopy, dog pens, water, cooler, and chairs to the far side of the ring. He saw that Storm's kennel pad was wet and tacky and so was his back.

"Have you noticed that Storm is sticky?" he asked Cassy.

"We had an accident. I spilled orange juice on him."

As the competition neared, Liam warmed up Storm over a practice jump. He heard a familiar voice behind him. "My, what a handsome dug. Is he a Lab?"

Olga doffed her stocking cap, revealing blond hair plastered tight to her head where her cap had been. Her otherwise loose jeans fit snugly in the wrong places, and her purple jacket seemed to be exploding on her ample body.

"He's a flat-coated retriever."

"Ooh! A bleck-coated retreefer. He looks like a bleck golden retreefer." Olga smiled and stroked Storm's head and back. She looked puzzled. "He feels steecky. Has he rolled in somethin'?"

"I think it's orange juice."

"He rolled on an orange?"

"Yes. That's it. Please excuse us. Our turn is coming."

"Ooh, I'm surry. Good luck."

Because of the interruption, Liam only had one minute to walk the first course and plan his strategy. He reviewed the course before entering the ring with Storm. The gate steward looked impatient and motioned him to begin.

Cool temperatures always had the same effect on Storm. He was wired as he ripped around the course. Unfortunately, after the eighth obstacle, he ran into a tunnel on the left instead of jumping a hurdle on the right. The judge held up both hands. Off course. Ten faults.

Olga offered consolation as he left the ring. "Ooh, that's too bad. You ver doing so well. Perheps you ver a leettel late on your call effter obstacle eight."

"I think that's it."

Olga responded cheerily, "You'll do better next time."

"Thanks."

The fog lifted shortly after nine. Liam slouched in a folding chair and stretched his legs. The sun felt good, and he was drifting toward sleep when he was jolted awake.

"Liam, how can you always take a morning nap at these trials. Aren't you even a little bit nervous?"

"When you're up at four on a Saturday morning, you need to catch up where you can."

"I see you have a new friend," Cassy said.

"What? Who?"

"That lady following you around today!"

"Oh, that's Olga. She chased us out of that ringside spot reserved for the food vendor. I think she's feeling guilty. She's going overboard to be nice to me."

"Yeah, I know what you mean. She asked me about your 'bleck-coated golden retreefer' earlier. She's in charge of awards and restrooms."

Liam stretched lazily. "Are you getting a little excited? Your turn is coming up."

"Not too bad. I just feel like throwing up."

A missed contact on the A-Frame cost Storm a qualifying score in the second event, and the next run was equally unsuccessful. After three runs they had no Qs. Cassy and Myst had also failed on their first three runs.

With some trepidation, Liam walked Storm toward the ring for their last event of the day. They warmed up near the ring where the food vendor was to have set up, but had never showed up.

"Good luck," came a voice from the sideline, sounding more like pity than encouragement.

"Thanks, Olga."

Storm was cautious in the early half of the course, but gradually increased speed as he neared the end and finished with no faults. They had a Q and were now one for four on the day.

"Ooh, that was wonderful!" whooped Olga, grinning from ear to ear. "Do you know we're going to award a High in Trial ribbon to the dug with the most qualifying runs this weekend? Your bleck dug should be eboot right up there."

"Thanks for the encouragement, but that was our first Q today. Surely, there must be a lot of dogs that have done better."

"Dear, you mustn't think like a wuss. Tomorrow is another day."

Liam just smiled. He planned to skip Sunday and catch the 49ers on TV instead of embarrassing himself. Visions of helmet-clad warriors racing up and down green fields drifted through his mind as he started the process of disassembling their camp.

Cassy and Myst returned from their last run. "What are you doing?"

"Today's been a disaster. Why don't we pack up and go home?"

"But we've paid for tomorrow. We're starting to get it together."

The helmet-clad warriors in Liam's vision turned gray, blurred, and dissipated. "Are there any doughnuts left?"

"I believe you ate the last six for lunch."

They took a ten-minute walk to the Burger King across the highway. By the time they returned it was dark, the fog was back, and at 8:30 they rolled out down sleeping bags in the van. Agility campers had a phrase for the night ahead: a three-dog night. Two people and only two dogs huddled closely together for warmth, bonded together in some prehistoric symbiotic relationship.

↬

Liam woke up and checked his watch. 6:00 a.m. Reluctantly, he got up and trudged through the fog toward the restroom. Each step on the frost-covered dry grass crackled as if he were walking on broken glass. Upon leaving the restroom, he noticed the sign above the door read "Women." He hoped the obscure figure he passed in the darkness hadn't noticed his faux pas.

The first event on Sunday was called Gamblers. In this event, handler and dog had a forty-second opening to ad-lib obstacles for points. The harder obstacles got more points. At the conclusion of the opening, a whistle indicated that the handler needed to send his dog over four obstacles twenty feet away, in the correct order and in fifteen seconds or less. The Gamble looked impossible. The handlers all grumbled as they walked the course. As the event proceeded, everyone had been failing.

This was Storm's favorite game. He enjoyed the opening because there were no faults, only points. Crazy fast could produce more points. The tunnels were as much fun as chasing squirrels. At full speed he could sometimes knock them loose from their moorings. The whistle sounded. Liam's voice went an octave higher, and Storm seemed to know he needed to help him out

"Out. Jump. Jump."

Storm moved away and cleared two jumps. Directly in his path was a tunnel.

"Tight!"

Storm looked disappointed, as if his squirrels had suddenly vanished, but he ignored the tunnel and turned toward Liam. Jump. Jump. What's next: a jump, weave poles, or a tunnel? Storm probably hoped it was the tunnel. Liam clapped his hands loudly, which meant weave poles and dinner. If Storm was fast enough, he could knock one of those sticks loose.

"Go on!"

Storm accelerated and cleared the last jump. He looked ready for a liver treat.

The small crowd peering through the fog was stunned. They broke into spontaneous cheering for the only team to make the Gamble that day. For the rest of the day, competitors whispered to their friends, "That's the guy who got the Gamble with the black dog."

Next came a speed event, all jumps and tunnels. The dogs needed to average five yards a second or more. Storm qualified again over his required twenty-four-inch-high jumps.

Liam and Storm were in the zone. Their bodies and minds were in perfect harmony. Their confidence bordered on arrogance. They became oblivious to everything around them, and their focus was absolute.

The third event was a Regular course with all the obstacles. Storm won for the second time on Sunday. Liam barely noticed Olga when he came off the course.

"Ooh, you're doing so well with Storm. You are now tied for first place!"

"Pardon? First place in what?"

"High in Trial. You have four qualifying rounds. Same as Mary Kay and her sheltie. The next round will decide everything."

Taken aback by this revelation, Liam asked, "What happens if we tie?"

"If you and Mary Kay have the same number of qualifying rounds, the tie breaker is first places. You are ahead two to one. There's a really nice ribbon for the winning team!"

The final event began at four. Storm needed one more clear round to be High in Trial. Liam was nervous and lost in thought. A booming voice broke his concentration.

"Your wife has her collie smoking up the courses oot there. Good luck!"

Liam didn't bother to correct her spousal mistake. "Thanks, Olga."

He caught glimpses of the smaller dogs running the last course of the weekend. Mary Kay's sheltie ran the course with jumps at sixteen inches. The dog and handler were poetry in motion, seemingly connected by an invisible string, a run so sweet it could rot teeth. As they approached the finish, Mary Kay raised her arms in triumph, distracting the sheltie so it ran around the last jump and crossed the finish line. Off course. Liam and Storm won by default, two first places to one.

Mary Kay stopped by Liam on her way out of the ring.

"Tough break," he said.

"That was my fault. I turned my shoulders too much. When you're done running, perhaps you could give me tips for doing Gambles and distance handling."

Olga beamed as she presented the High in Trial ribbon to the winner. She gave Liam a big suffocating hug. "We hope to see you again next year," she said.

He gasped for air. "Wouldn't miss it."

Driving home, Cassy laughed about Storm smelling like orange juice. She related Olga's story about a man who got lost in the women's restroom on Sunday morning. While Cassy dozed, Liam listened to the last quarter of Sunday night football on the car radio, but he couldn't concentrate on the game. He kept reliving Storm's triumph in the Gamble. He didn't care that traffic was backed up on Highway 101 because people were Christmas shopping.

18 Back into the Fog

What little cat feet?
Carl Sandburg never saw
This Lioness linger.

Winter nights in Sonoma County are longer and colder than the neighboring San Francisco Bay area. Cold wet air trapped under warmer upper air produces a pronounced inversion layer. The tule fog, named after the grass wetlands of the Central Valley, creeps across the Delta and spills damp and chilly air into the Valley of the Moon, thick as a gray blanket, like the fake fog in horror movies. For those driving, it's like sticking your head into a bucket of milk.

Late Sunday night, Liam said goodbye to Cassy and drove carefully along Highway 12 toward Santa Rosa through the thick fog. The house in Santa Rosa had been sold, and to save some money he'd moved to a small rental cottage with one bedroom and one bath. He was now legally divorced. The impending day in court on drug possession was always in the back of his mind.

He had become the weekend darling of a diminutive Northern California agility world. By some standards, this might not have been enough basis for his euphoric mood, but he was also in love. The thick gray fog oppressing his life finally seemed to be lifting.

Liam recalled another foggy day when he was a freshman at San Francisco State. Two gigantic oil tankers had collided in San Francisco Bay, spilling more than 800,000 gallons of thick, black, gooey oil. A northern current pushed the slick back through the Golden Gate, where it clung to shores and beaches up and down the central coast. He and three friends cut classes and helped rescue birds trapped in the sludge in Bolinas Lagoon.

His youthful idealism hadn't died, he now realized, simply faded. Sometimes, young people in the eighties made a 180-degree turn from wearing flowers in their hair to wiggling in a St. Vitus dance of materialism. He'd married Myra and grown complacent while gathering the trappings of suburban life on their two incomes.

Myra's friends were getting rich, pouring their money into landed property, investing in mysterious strategies called leveraging, wrap-around loans, and bundled mortgages. They smoked a little pot, but the baby boomers' smart drug of choice was real estate, producing the high that comes with wealth. Liam had listened absently to their conversations, politely nodded his head, and wondered if the 49ers could win that week.

When he needed help and money, he'd turned to Myra, who bailed him out of his nightmare experience. He felt guilty. He hadn't bothered to return her phone calls.

Liam parked the van and didn't bother to leash Storm as they headed for the front door. He fumbled for his key, and when he couldn't find it immediately, absently tried the door, which turned out to be unlocked. He was too tired to wonder why.

Not only had he left the front door unlocked, but the cottage lights were lit as well. Storm bolted down the hall into the bathroom. He was probably thirsty, and Liam kept a water bowl in the bathroom to keep his dog from drinking out of the toilet. He was jolted to reality when he heard a familiar woman's voice talking to his dog.

He entered the bathroom. Storm had his front feet parked on the tub, his tail wagging energetically.

Splish-Splash, Myra's in the bath. The nonsense rhyme ran quickly through Liam's head.

"Come on in," she said.

"Holy Toledo. You surprised me." He did a U-turn. "I'll shut the door."

"Don't be silly. It's not like you've haven't seen me undressed before."

"I'll wait in the living room."

When Liam and Myra met, they were both naked in a hot tub, attending a National Science Foundation Summer Institute at Sonoma State. Eight weeks of inspired learning and numerous "hands on" field trips throughout Northern California had the teachers totally energized about the subject of ecology. After a field trip to the coastal tide pools, the instructor invited the participants to camp out at his vacation home in Mendocino. The evening ecology lecture was followed by a reenactment of "Teachers Gone Wild."

It all started out innocently enough. The ladies and gentlemen took turns au-naturel in the sauna, followed by a 100-yard streak to a hot tub, during which the opposite sex cheered them on. Finally, the sauna-hot tub routine became a co-ed activity. When one of the Minnesota participants later confessed to his wife, she complained to Senator Hubert Humphrey about what she perceived to be a waste of taxpayers' money. Liam and most of the participants defended the program during a follow-up inquiry that came to nothing. The Sonoma State Institute survived for many years afterward as one of the most popular destinations for science teachers.

Myra taught science before attending that NSF Institute, but decided to take up real estate a year later. They kept in touch and were married in 1978.

She emerged from Liam's bathroom wrapped in a large beach towel. "I hope you're not angry. I've been collecting a stack of your mail that got forwarded to me. It's on the kitchen table. I tried to call you a few times, but you never answer."

"I'm really sorry about that. I've been meaning to get back to you. I appreciated your help when I needed it."

"I thought we could celebrate the felony charges being dropped. So we're friends?"

"Of course."

She sat down, adjusted her towel, and crossed her legs. "So how was your weekend?"

"Fantastic. Storm won the High in Trial ribbon."

"Sounds wonderful. Anything else?"

"Well…the fog on the drive to Madera was awful. It's spilled into Sonoma County tonight."

"I suppose I should be on my way. I don't look forward to driving home."

Liam paused before replying. "Look, we're both adults here. It's too dangerous to drive anywhere right now. You can stay in the bedroom. I'll sleep on the couch."

"I don't want to put you to any trouble. Are you sure?"

"Why not? You can wear a pair of my pajamas. Don't be surprised if Storm jumps up on the bed."

She laughed. "You can join me if you like."

He hesitated. Surely that was meant to be a joke. "That's probably not a good idea. I'm really tired. Let me know if you need anything."

"Okay." Myra smiled. "Good night."

Liam got a pillow and blanket and settled down on the couch. He was about to fall asleep when he heard Storm trot into the bedroom and jump onto the bed.

Early next morning, he woke to the telephone ringing. Instinctively, he reached for the receiver on the nightstand next to the bed and his hand met empty air. Now fully awake, he realized he was on the couch.

He heard Myra's voice in the bedroom. "He's still asleep. Can I take a message? Yes, he's fine. Should I have him call you? Okay. Goodbye."

Liam sat up, his heart pounding. "Who was that?"

"She said her name was Cassy. She wanted to know if you drove home safely last night. I told her yes. She said it wasn't necessary to call her back."

19 Blood-sucking Parasites

In December, Liam was convicted of misdemeanor drug possession and placed on probation. He agreed with his lawyer to appeal and wondered if the nightmare would ever end.

The following month, the Sonoma County hilltops received a blanket of snow. The weather turned unusually cold, as frigid as the reception he received in Sebastopol the day after the fiasco with Myra. Yes, Cassy completely accepted his explanation. Yes, his ex-wife showed up unexpectedly, and it would have been unwise for her to drive home in the thick fog. Yes, he slept on the couch. Unfortunately, Cassy would be quite busy for a while. She was registered for a full spring schedule at Sonoma State. The dog agility had been fun, but the time had come to take responsibility for her future. She needed a time out.

Liam still had one friend in that frigid house. Ben told him to wait a few weeks. Take up a new hobby. As the days grew longer, the ice might thaw.

Whenever Liam walked Storm past the local tennis courts, his dog would pull hard on the leash and plunge into the bushes. Ten times out of ten, he'd emerge with an old tennis ball and demand a fetch game. In a eureka moment, Liam decided his new hobby would be tracking.

A week later, at 6:45 on a frigid morning, six handlers and their dogs gathered in the local community college parking lot for their first tracking lesson. A glimmer of light in the southeast promised relief from the freezing temperature. Five of the six dogs sat politely in a heel position next to their masters. The sixth strained to strike up an unwanted acquaintance with a demure golden retriever. Liam smiled apologetically and told Storm, "Lie down."

Storm lay down and panted clouds of white steam.

A portly lady dropped a liver snap from her mouth directly into the jaws of the object of Storm's affection. "Good girl, Dawn." She turned to address the owner of the unruly retriever. "I'm so thrilled. Dawn earned her CD title this weekend, and she's only three."

Liam wasn't quite sure what that meant, but it sounded important, so he congratulated her and gave her a high five. She told him her name was Betty.

"That's wonderful!" said a small middle-aged man with a large dog. His black mustache matched the color of his dog. "I'm Norman. Rembrandt got his CD at two years of age and his CDX at three. I'm almost as proud as the day he earned his show dog Champion title. He's a Bouvier. You know, like in *The Dog of Flanders*."

Liam yawned.

Norman studied Storm. "That's a flat-coated retriever. I've seen them at dog shows."

"Yes, that's right. This is Storm."

"Have you done conformation?"

"Conformation? No, we haven't done the show dog thing. He does some agility."

"Agility. Oh, that's nice. Have you tried obedience? Rembrandt has a CDX in obedience."

"I think you mentioned that a moment ago. We've just done the sit, stay, come stuff." Storm rolled onto his back and wiggled.

"Oh," said Norman, "that's nice."

At seven sharp, Elizabeth, the tracking teacher, began the lesson. She was young and athletic-looking, the kind of person you couldn't keep up with on a backpacking trip. "Dogs can follow dead skin flakes, sweat droplets, and scent mists," she explained. "They move their noses in such a way that exhaled air deflects through slits on the sides of their noses. That way, outgoing air doesn't mix or dilute the scented air streaming into their nostrils. They have twenty to forty times more olfactory receptors than humans. Some dogs can detect scents a million times better than humans." She looked around at the group. "Let's move to the lawn. I want you to divide yourselves into groups of two."

Two elderly women paired up while a group of three that included Norman debated who should remain. When Norman became the odd man out, Elizabeth suggested that he and Rembrandt pair with Liam and Storm.

After walking to a grassy area, the instructor gave instructions. "One partner will lay the track, and the other will work their dog."

"Can I be first?" asked Norman.

"First at laying the track or working your dog?"

"Either one. I want to do the harder part."

"Liam," Elizabeth said, "Would you lay the track? Leave your scented glove at the finish. Norman and Rembrandt can track first."

Liam moved to the starting point. For this beginning exercise, he shuffled his feet to leave the maximum scent possible. He then placed a flag next to his left heel and dropped a hot dog slice. Next, he moved straight ahead, pacing off fifty steps before placing another flag and food. He repeated this procedure a few more times and finally dropped a glove containing a half-dozen hot dog slices. He moved forward for several seconds and circled back to the start, being careful not to leave a new scent near the track he had laid.

Rembrandt would be tracking Liam's scent. Norman snapped a harness and ten feet of line on his dog and commanded, "Track!" The Bouvier rushed to the first flag, found the food reward, and started moving slowly ahead with his nose to the ground, sniffing purposefully.

Norman looked to Elizabeth for approval. "Are we doing this right?"

"Yes. Keep a little more tension on the line."

Rembrandt moved straight as an arrow to the next flag and quickly dispatched the food reward.

"Elizabeth, how soon do you think we'll be ready for our TD test?"

"That's hard to tell."

Liam whispered to Betty. "What's a TD?"

"That's a touchdown. No, just kidding. It's the Tracking Dog title. The TDX would be the next step. X stands for excellent."

"Thanks."

Rembrandt moved forward again, but veered suddenly to the left. The sudden unexpected tension on the line caught Norman by surprise. "No! No! Over here."

The Bouvier ignored the command and sniffed a gopher hole near a pine tree. He peed on the tree, but with some coaxing, found the track again. A moment later, Rembrandt found Liam's glove and made short work of the hot dog slices.

"How was that, Elizabeth?"

"Good for the first time."

Norman beamed with pride. He moved to a new area to lay a track for Storm. "Is this right, Elizabeth? Should I drop one hot dog slice or two?"

Elizabeth took a deep breath. "One should do it."

While Norman continued his task, Liam watched Betty and her golden retriever work the track her partner had laid. Dawn looked eager and moved quickly, her nose barely skimming the ground. She picked up the glove, sat at attention, and received lavish praise from Betty.

When it was Storm's turn, Liam struggled to attach the harness. This proved only slightly easier than untangling Christmas tree lights. One of four openings needed to fit over Storm's head. He guessed wrong twice, but eventually snapped the apparatus around Storm's chest, attached the tracking line, and moved to the start. As they were about to begin, Elizabeth noticed Liam had missed one of his dog's legs when he put on the harness.

"Can I show him how to do it?" pleaded Norman, who hurried over to provide uninvited assistance.

Liam stepped to the side to block Norman. "Let me see if I can figure this out." His task proved difficult because Storm grew impatient and rolled around on his back. After two more attempts, the harness was attached correctly.

"Track!" Liam commanded.

Storm snatched the first hot dog slice and ran at full speed to the second food drop nearly pulling Liam off his feet. Barely hesitating, the dog gulped each food reward in sequence, and raced to Norman's glove, where he finished off the hot dogs in record time. He picked up the glove and shook it as hard as he could. The entire exercise took about ten seconds.

Norman shook his head, "I don't think Storm was really tracking. Isn't he supposed to smell the ground?"

"Yes," Elizabeth said. "But usually a track is an hour old or more and is on the ground. Today the tracks are so fresh there are air scents. Storm probably air-scented the hot dogs rather than tracking Norman's scent."

Norman beamed after correctly identifying the tracking anomaly.

To close the session, Elizabeth gathered the group together. "In our next lesson, we'll use tracks that have aged for an hour."

After five lessons at the campus, the class met early one morning in the foothills east of Santa Rosa. The sun came up, illuminating wide-open fields over hilly terrain. It was cold, and Liam wished he'd remembered to bring gloves. There was one more problem. Elizabeth warned the class that ticks were everywhere.

Liam knew something about ticks. They can really get under your skin. They're stealth biters. Some carry Lyme disease, and they're ubiquitous in California's wild places. Smart hikers wear boots, tuck their pants in, and spray themselves with foul-smelling substances. Even then a few may get past this first line of defense.

Liam wore light-colored clothing so he could see if any black bodies were crawling on his pants. Ticks are not particular, and enjoy pets as well. Remarkable chemical breakthroughs protect dogs from fleas and ticks. They keep ticks from biting, but the parasites will still hitch a ride while looking for more promising hosts, like humans. The tracklayers couldn't use chemicals because they interfered with the tracking scents.

At this point in the training, the tracks were more than four hundred yards long and included three right-angle turns. They had to age an hour before they were used. After the tracks had been laid, the class walked to the crest of a hill to wait.

Liam admired the sweeping views. Heavy December rains had produced thick new green grass. In the distance, two white-tailed kites hovered in the air a hundred feet away, flapping their wings furiously before dive-bombing on unsuspecting prey.

Elizabeth explained the activities for the day. There were many questions, mostly from Norman. Liam checked his pants regularly for moving black specks. Storm inched closer to the object of his affection, but Dawn looked away and ignored him. Twenty minutes later, even Norman was getting antsy.

"Elizabeth, can I tell a joke?"

She looked surprised. "Okay. Go ahead."

"What happened when the werewolf swallowed an alarm clock?"

"I give up. What happened?"

"He got ticks!" Norman appeared to enjoy his joke and made rhythmic guttural noises that Liam took for laughter. An elderly lady giggled. Liam checked his pants.

Norman, apparently flush with the success of his first riddle asked, "Liam, what's the difference between a lawyer and a tick?"

Liam remembered this bad joke from his science classes. "A tick is a blood-sucking parasite that leaves you when you die. A lawyer is a—"

Norman feigned a look of disappointment and interrupted. "Oh, you've heard that one before, haven't you? By the way, there's a tick on your pants," warned Norman.

Liam bent forward slowly and checked each leg. If I panic and there's no tick, he thought, Norman will surely have a good laugh. "I think you're mistaken," he said.

"No, I'm serious. It's crawling toward your crotch."

Liam faced a universal male dilemma, wondering if his fly was unzipped in mixed company. But the thought of a tick actually heading toward this sensitive area was overpowering. Once again, he looked between his legs, thinking Norman must be ready to explode into laughter at any moment. He bent further and saw it—black, enormous, with eight legs—moving directly toward his zipper.

"Yikes!" Liam flicked it with his finger and it was gone, off to one of those mysterious hiding places that ticks go to, like the caves in Afghanistan that harbor terrorists.

Norman made gurgling guttural noises.

Over the next month, Liam and Storm continued training. Some days, the retriever was a regular Sherlock Holmes and moved directly to the end-tracking article. Other days, he was more like Inspector Clouseau, the bumbling detective in the Pink Panther movies.

When Elizabeth determined her students were ready for their first official tracking test, she explained the process. Two weeks before the test, a random draw of potential entrants around the state determined who would be allowed to enter. There were eleven entries, but only six openings. Storm's entry was lucky to be chosen, as well as that of Betty and her golden retriever, Dawn. Norman was crushed when

Rembrandt missed the cut, but they became the first alternate. When one of the entrants from Southern California withdrew two days before the test, Rembrandt was added to the field.

Quarter-mile tracks with flags were laid the day before the test. The entrants were not allowed to be present. Early on the morning of the trial, before the entrants arrived, the course setters re-walked the course, removing all the flags except the first two. The end article would be a wallet. Dogs at the start line were allowed to smell a sock with the same scent as the wallet. The rules allowed water for the dog on the course, but no food.

Saturday morning, the trackers gathered in the Palo Alto Foothills Park, and the start times were drawn at random. Two judges, a middle-aged man and an elderly woman, reviewed the rules for the handlers, who had no idea where the tracks led. They needed to trust their dog's keen sense of smell. Broken dry weeds gave the handlers occasional clues, but if they blatantly directed the dog, they would fail.

Elizabeth attended to give her students support. "This is a cattle ranch, and the cows are curious. They may investigate and pee on the flags, or maybe leave a pile of manure. It could throw your dogs off the scent."

"That's not fair," complained Norman.

Dawn drew the first start time; Storm was second, and Rembrandt sixth. The earlier start times got a fresher track. As the day wore on, time and breezes would make the tracking more difficult.

"I can't go sixth," lamented Norman. "Because I was an alternate, I made a doctor's appointment this afternoon."

"On Saturday?" Liam asked.

"Yes, it was the only time available for a month. Remember when I warned you about that the tick? You owe me one. Change start times with me."

Liam paused a moment. "Okay."

Swapping start times required extenuating circumstances. After extensive pleading by Norman, the judges allowed the change.

Betty and Dawn were first. Dawn was brilliant. She never wavered and moved to the end article in less than fifteen minutes. She sat at attention with the wallet in her mouth. The two judges happily announced that she had passed.

Betty squealed and gave her golden a big hug.

Norman and Rembrandt were next. The new smells distracted Rembrandt, but Norman was determined and applied gentle pressure on the line to keep his dog on task. Norman's handling bordered on guiding his dog and nearly caused his elimination. After twenty minutes, Norman cheered when Rembrandt picked up the wallet.

"Pass!" exclaimed the judges.

As Norman pulled a water bottle from his pack to give Rembrandt a drink, a folded paper fell from his pocket.

The elderly woman judge stooped to pick it up. "You dropped something." She frowned as she unfolded the paper. "This is a map of today's courses. How did you get this?"

An ashen-faced Norman replied, "Oh no, it's an old map."

The judge persisted. "This map has today's six tracks on it."

Norman did his best to explain, but only dug himself deeper into disgrace. A bystander stepped forward. "I noticed someone yesterday with a pair of binoculars. His car had a bumper sticker that said, "My Bouvier is Smarter than Your Honor Student."

Norman was disqualified. Despite this unsavory turn of events, the trial continued.

At ten o'clock, the last team of the day began the test. As goofy as Storm might be in practice, he became the consummate competitor. Aware of the spectators, he fed off the excitement. The track was near the two-hour age limit.

Liam took a deep breath and put the dog's harness on correctly the first try. As they moved to the first flag, he let out several feet of line. He would not be allowed to get any closer than twenty feet during the test. "Track!" he commanded.

Storm moved forward, his nose to the ground. He reached the second flag at thirty yards. There were no more flags. After a hundred yards, he stopped, and retreated a few steps. Liam reeled in the slack line and maintained light tension. Storm had probably overshot the scent, but picked it up again and turned left. He moved quickly, nose to the ground, until a mouse scurried through the grass.

Liam softly admonished, "Leave it."

Storm went back to work, but hesitated eighty yards farther along, near a pile of cow manure. Perhaps the course setter had placed a flag there earlier, indicating a turn. A few feet away, the grass was flattened. Had an animal lain there recently, or were those the footprints of the tracklayer? Liam allowed Storm to sniff. The dog lifted his leg and peed on the manure. In agility, they'd be disqualified for that, but this was acceptable behavior in tracking. He moved tentatively to the right, then more aggressively, appearing to have regained the scent on the third leg. The wind was blowing harder.

Storm kept his nose to the ground, snorting air in and out of his nostrils. He turned to the left on what may have been the final turn. He hesitated a few times, searching back and forth, then moved ahead five yards, picked up a brown wallet in his mouth, and began wiggling all over. An adrenalin rush coursed through Liam's body. He took the wallet, turned to the judges fifty yards back, and waved it frantically over his head.

"Pass!" shouted the elderly woman judge. "Yes, pass," agreed the other.

Storm's teacher, Elizabeth, beamed, and offered congratulations to her two students who had earned TD's. "I think the wind helped today. It blew away the air scents and made Storm concentrate on the ground."

She glanced at Liam. "There's a tick crawling on your jacket sleeve."

He casually flicked it into the brush.

20 The Hound of Bakersfield

Storm could smell water. His breed had developed from the Newfoundland, the legendary black giants who saved drowning Vikings from watery deaths. The dog in the Peter Pan story was a Newfie. Their webbed feet make them powerful swimmers, and they use their tails as rudders. Their rescue instincts are most acute when children or other family members are floundering in the water.

Liam saw these ancestral qualities in his dog. He'd heard that Storm swam to his own rescue through the Florida floodwaters following Hurricane Andrew. The rescuers reported that he plunged in and began swimming so powerfully that his shoulders extended well above the surface of the water.

In early March Liam drove Storm to a tracking test near Lake Isabella in Southern California. He was thinking about Cassy. He heard she was training Myst again for agility. Maybe if he took a break from tracking, they could reconnect.

He passed through arid, flat agricultural land decorated with oil rigs, their rocker arms swinging up and down like mechanized prehistoric birds. Country music playing on the radio helped ease the tedium of the long drive from Santa

Rosa. He passed Oildale, a hardscrabble suburb of Bakersfield, the boyhood home of Merle Haggard.

Floods had plagued Bakersfield until the 1950's, when the Isabella Dam was built to control the spring snowmelt from Mt. Whitney. Bakersfield quickly changed from a springtime swamp to a city of more than half a million. This dubious metamorphosis followed a deal that allowed Kern River water to be appropriated for extensive agricultural uses in the central valley.

Leaving Highway 99, Liam turned east on 178. The ugly duckling landscape was gradually transformed into a breathtaking wild vista. The road twisted high above the Lower Kern River, and had a name as well as a number. Kern Canyon Road meandered easterly through the Sequoia National Forest.

He camped Friday evening in the National Forest, and next morning drove to the tracking site. Storm drew fifth position. The sixth and last spot went to a bloodhound.

Liam knew from his tracking classes that bloodhounds are nature's finest detectives. Even in an age of electronic surveillance, police have discovered that the wet nose of a bloodhound is the best equipment money can buy. Their noses are reported to be three million times more sensitive than a human's. Unfortunately, bloodhounds have fallen out of favor with police forces. Despite their forensic skills at tracking suspects, they are hopeless at arresting them.

While watching the early trackers, Liam found himself talking to the man with the bloodhound.

"Mani Padilla," the young man introduced himself.

He looked to be in his twenties and very fit. His blue eyes contrasted with his swarthy complexion. Something about him looked familiar. "You should do well today. You've got the dog for it."

The bloodhound shook his head vigorously, dislodging the slobber hanging from his mouth. Loose folds of skin acted like a slingshot, flinging the saliva twenty feet. "Sherlock has a good nose," said Mani, "but he's a little erratic."

"Are you from this area?" Liam asked.

"Born here. Grandma and Grandpa came from Oklahoma in the thirties. They thought they were coming to 'the land of milk and honey.' Mom met Dad in the fields."

The day before, Liam had seen the ramshackle housing for migrant farm workers. Somehow, each new wave of immigrants found a way to survive. Liam had grown up in the bungalow belt on Chicago's West Side, near the Projects. His grandfather told stories about his father, who came from Ireland and worked on rail crews for the Great Northern Railroad. The other workers despised the floods of Irish immigrants and called them dumb Micks. Many Chicago Irish worked at the Stockyards, where waste was dumped into the Chicago River, which became known as the "Stinking River." This garbage flowed into Lake Michigan, where it mixed with the city's drinking water. After numerous outbreaks of typhoid, city engineers, in something of an engineering miracle, reversed the river flow and sent Chicago's waste downstate.

The Annual St. Patrick's Day parade, often led by an Irish mayor, was the biggest day of the year for kids in Liam's neighborhood. Gramps marched with the firemen, Dad with the policemen. In a crowning touch, the City dyed the Chicago River green.

Liam's father had a spotless reputation on the force as an honest cop. He really cared about the people on his beat. During the 1968 Democratic Convention, young people from around the country came to Chicago to protest the Vietnam

War. Ordered to dispel the crowds and beat demonstrators, he refused and was suspended.

The family moved to Northern California, and Liam's father struggled at odd jobs. His older brother, Sean, became an air flight controller at San Francisco International. The family's hard luck continued in 1981 when the Controllers Union went on strike. The President fired the strikers and banned them from federal service for life. Sean and his parents emigrated to Ireland. Liam had recently married and stayed behind at his teaching job in Santa Rosa.

The bloodhound lay down and fell asleep. Even when awake, Liam could barely see his eyes, nearly hidden by huge wrinkled folds of skin. Long floppy ears stir up dust and scent that can be trapped in those wrinkles.

"May I ask why you picked a bloodhound?" Liam asked.

"Well, I'd like to get into law enforcement. Passed all the tests, but can't get a job. I found Sherlock at the Shelter, and I've been volunteering in Search and Rescue, trying to get noticed by someone with clout."

"Well, you look fit enough. How do you keep in shape?"

"Running."

"Now I remember. You ran at Bakersfield High. Won the state cross country finals in 1990."

"Yeah, but it was '92, and I came in second. Got nosed out at the finish."

"Did you run in college?"

"A year at the community college, but I had to work. Our family had eight mouths to feed."

"You'd have been a great college runner. Sorry you didn't get the opportunity."

When Storm's turn came, he was quickly confused and had trouble getting on track. Liam passed footprints in the tall grass on the right, but Storm charged straight ahead. It was hopeless. He waited for the judge to blow her whistle. Five minutes later, she did.

Sherlock was next. He appeared to catch an air scent and moved confidently into a pasture until he became tangled in a wire fence. The bloodhound's sense of smell was suspect, and his sight left something to be desired. He freed himself, but a moment later bumped into a post with enough force to knock a human silly. The whistle came quickly for Sherlock.

Liam offered his condolences. "Tough break. Sherlock seemed so confident."

"We've had a little success in Search and Rescue training. All I could do today was point to the ground and pray."

A beeping noise interrupted their conversation. Mani checked his pager and walked to the parking area to find a phone. Five minutes later he returned.

"A little boy wandered away from a campground near here. They want me to help find him."

"Anything I can do to help?"

"Thanks. Follow me. Maybe you can help in the search."

Twenty minutes later, they reached the staging area at the Carrizo Plain campground. The nearby river flowed relatively flat, making it a favorite jumping off point for rafters and kayakers.

Sheriff Lucas Griffin, looking for all the help he could muster, allowed Liam and Storm to join the search. Lucas, a giant of a man with a dark bushy mustache and ruddy complexion, appeared not to have missed many meals. His belly hid his belt except for an enormous buckle. He briefed the search and rescue crew. "The parents believe their son, Billy Santana, may have been headin' toward the river. They last saw him about nine this morning, so he's been missin' four hours. He's eight years old and wearin' a tan jacket.

"I want three teams to search east along the main trail, and the other three to search west. Every four hundred yards or so, we'll send a dog team toward the river. Billy's mom loaned us the socks he wore yesterday to be used for scent. Remember, this is a mean piece of water. We've got a Class V rapids a mile down the river to the west. More than 200 lives have been lost here since 1968. If you spot the boy, blow a whistle."

Mani and Liam searched the west sector. The other teams had German shepherds. Those dogs were not only good trackers, but they could "finish" if the object of the search happened to be a fugitive.

One by one, dog-handler teams entered the search area and moved toward the river. Lucas held Billy's sock in front of the bloodhound, which seemed more interested in sniffing Lucas's crotch. Mani looped a rope over his left shoulder and led his dog off the main trail on a footpath. Sherlock lifted his head, sniffed the air, and quickly circled back to sniff Lucas's crotch.

Lucas deadpanned, "We gotta' stop meetin' like this. I'm notcher type."

Mani, red-faced, led Sherlock back to the footpath, where he wandered around aimlessly before running into a tree.

After continuing along the main trail for another quarter mile, Lucas showed the sock to Storm, who grabbed it and began a tug of war. Lucas sighed and directed them to the final search area.

Thirty minutes later, all Storm had discovered was a covey of quail. Liam had to constantly stop him from browsing on the lush new grass. A fire had swept through the area a few years earlier, and the ugly, charred remains were feeding new growth in the warm spring weather. Bright green grass and fiery orange poppies contrasted with the new dark green foliage of the oaks. Liam tried to imagine how it must have looked to explorer John Fremont when he crossed the Sierra at this point in the 1840's.

He was jolted back to reality when he heard a whistle. Sherlock was baying loudly over the roar of the nearby rapids. Off to the right, Liam saw the bloodhound. His tracking line taut, he strained to move toward the last relatively level part of the river. Farther to the left, the river changed into a raging mass of white water before disappearing into Kern Canyon.

Moving as fast as possible toward the shore, Liam spotted a small boy wearing a tan jacket trapped on a sandbar in the middle of the river. Moments later, he joined Mani at the river's edge. Liam struggled to hold Storm back from the water and decided to tie him to a nearby tree.

"Billy! Stay put! We're coming to help!" Mani shouted over the deafening river noise. "Stay there! La estancia puso!" The boy either couldn't hear or didn't understand, because he moved toward the water.

"How did he get out there?" Liam asked.

"My guess is he fell in the river upstream and hauled out on that sandbar. Must be cold. That water's freezing."

Mani removed his shoes and pants and tied the rope around his waist. "I'm going in. You stay here and secure the loose end." As he moved to the river's edge, the boy moved slowly off the sandbar, slipped, and was swept downstream by the current. "Dammit! We've got to get him before he gets sucked into the rapids."

As they ran downstream, Storm strained to free himself. He pulled free of his collar and plunged into the river.

Swimming strongly, he reached the Billy and grabbed the boy's jacket collar in his mouth. Storm tried to swim back to shore, but he was in a stalemate with the river's strong current and could make no progress.

Mani sprinted to a position downstream and waded into the river until the water level reached his chest. Several seconds later, he seized the boy's jacket. Storm kept his hold. Liam planted his feet and pulled with all his strength, struggling to hold his ground and acting as the focal point of a roped arc that swung the trio through the river toward shore. Only a few feet from safety, Storm lost his grip on the boy's jacket. Once again, he fought with all his reserves to keep from drifting downstream into the watery maelstrom. He struggled valiantly, but looked exhausted.

Mani hoisted the boy onto the riverbank and immediately jumped back into the cold water. With superhuman effort he reached Storm and put his arm around the dog's body. Liam's hands were burning, but he held onto the rope as man and dog arced back to the riverbank only a few feet from the rapids. Storm staggered ashore. Extending a hand, Liam pulled Mani out of the water. Not a word passed between them, but they felt an instant bond. They shook hands and proceeded to tend to Billy and their dogs. Liam took off his jacket and wrapped it around Storm, who was still shaking from his experience in the cold water.

"Gracias," murmured Billy.

"Su nada," Mani said.

Liam helped Billy out of his soaked shirt and transferred his own jacket from Storm to the boy. Storm licked Billy's face. The boy turned away shyly and smiled. "Buen perro."

One at a time, the other searchers joined the scene. Half an hour later, the boy was reunited with his tearful parents.

Lucas lavished praise on the rescuers and their dogs. He'd been looking for a bilingual deputy and told Mani to apply for work the following week. Sherlock had become more than a source of humor that day. Liam hoped the bloodhound would become a regular participant in future searches.

That afternoon on the drive home, he stopped in the San Joaquin Delta to watch a crop duster spraying an irrigated cotton field. On the other side of the highway, a group of farm workers picked asparagus. The men wore overalls, long-sleeved shirts, and hats to protect them from the sun. In smooth fast movements they walked through the fields, stooping to pick stems. They used knives to slice the ends off the stalks in one quick, strong motion, and dropped them into wicker baskets belted to their waists. When the baskets were full, they walked over to shallow yellow bins at the end of the rows and carefully transferred the asparagus from their baskets to the bins. Then they walked back into the field to stoop, pick, cut, and basket some more.

In a different decade these workers might have been Mani's parents or grandparents. They'd spent invisible lives doing the best they could to support their families. Maybe some day Bakersfield would have a parade. A dark-haired mayor with swarthy skin might lead firemen and policemen through the streets, third and fourth generation Americans who had their roots in these fields.

As Liam drove home, he turned on the radio and hit the seek button, finding a country music station. He listened to the end of "Kern River," a Merle Haggard song. He reached down and stroked Storm, sleeping next to him.

21 Losers

Cassy O'Neal felt confident...some of the time. At other times, she saw her life slipping away. She felt her life had direction, except on those days she seemed to have lost her way. She wanted to save the planet, but had trouble saving herself. Success was too often followed by failure. A college degree produced unemployment. She had worked part time as a waitress in Eureka before spending a month nestled in the branches of a 2000-year-old tree, but the tree was harvested anyway. Her former boyfriend sold grass and crank and wouldn't get out of her life. Her mother had fled to Alaska without telling her, and she had never known her father.

She could be moody and introspective, but the keys to unlocking her past and freeing her future might be closer than ever. She'd known her grandmother for a while, even though she didn't realize it at the time. Her step-grandfather had given her a home when she was about to become homeless. He had become a rock in her life, someone she could trust. He told her not to give up on Liam, whose story about a foggy night might yet become clear. She often thought about Liam. She wished she could believe him.

While walking Myst one morning, it came to her in an epiphany. She assessed her skills and her biggest asset, her companion at the other end of the leash. She resumed agility training and, during spring break at Sonoma State, entered the California Cup Championships in San Jose.

At the end of day one of the California Cup, Cassy O'Neil scanned the posted scores. She could hardly believe it. Myst was in second place, only five points out of first. Only a total collapse could deny her a medal and one of the top three positions. Cassy's mood bounced between euphoric and sick with anxiety.

She wanted to shake her loser self-image as the barefoot bastard daughter of a brain-fried hippie who grew up in New Mexico, the outcast high school girl without designer jeans, the girl who watched a redwood tree sawed down after living in its branches for a month.

Abigail Menke shifted her weight from left to right as she studied the scores. Her tethered six-year-old golden retriever stood panting at her side, alert and ready for action.

This was Abigail's first California Cup. Fifty pounds overweight and fifty years old, she didn't look like an athlete. The last one chosen in high school gym classes, the embarrassing softball player at family picnics, and the unsuccessful participant of numerous diet plans, Abigail found success in an unexpected field: dog agility. Her dog, Dreamer, was an athlete. Oh, he wouldn't beat the border collies and Aussies on a regular basis, but he may have been the best damn golden retriever anyone had ever seen. He was AKC royalty and had all those titles and hieroglyphics attached to his registered name.

At eighty dollars for six group lessons, it didn't come cheap. Abigal had been a steady customer for three years.

One hundred an hour for private lessons, so many sessions she lost track. She got a bargain on used equipment, a measly $3,000 and renovated her back yard into her training field of dreams. She spent more for vet, acupuncture, and chiropractor bills for the dog than her own medical insurance. She thanked God for that insurance. She wore braces on both knees and needed to schedule surgery after this championship trial.

The entry fees for a weekend of trialing ran close to a hundred. She didn't bother keeping track of the gas and motel bills anymore. They started on plastic and ended in never-never land. It didn't matter. She was addicted, a junkie, juiced on adrenaline, good at something for the first time in her life. She decorated her rumpus room with ribbons, certificates, and trophies.

She rationalized her addiction. Didn't she always keep the Christmas weekend and Thanksgiving free for family? And, after all, didn't her husband spend as much time and money on golf? Most of their vacations were planned around golf in some exotic spot.

Her husband had come to grips with Abigail's expenses, but not the forty weekends a year away from home, plus classes and private lessons two days a week. There were pricey seminars with the big names in the sport, and eight hundred dollars for the four-day Power Control Agility Camp. The presenters had been to the World Championships in Europe, appeared on television, and achieved cult status. Abigail wanted to be on television: the *Incredible Dog Challenge*, The *Outdoor Games*, the *AKC Nationals*, maybe a spot on the local news. Why not dream big? It was a long shot, but maybe, just maybe, someday she'd make the U.S. World Team.

Finally, her husband put his foot down. "You need to spend more time at home," he told her. "This doggie stuff has gotten out of hand. Make a choice—dog agility or me."

She chose Dreamer. Her husband moved out that weekend. She suspected he had a new love interest, anyway. Abigail cried and lost sleep for a while. She needed to repair her self-esteem, win some ribbons, and get an adrenaline fix. She entered the California Cup.

The ladies loved Preston Wadsworth, a tall, lean, handsome bachelor. He and his powerful blue merle, Ringo, looked like they were attached by an invisible umbilical cord as they snaked around courses. They were the only team that regularly beat the border collies.

Preston was supremely confident. He and the Aussie were the class of the field and led after the first day. They had a series of clean runs and were clearly the fastest team in the competition.

Preston had quit his civil engineering job four years earlier to pursue the new sport. He'd made more money at Bechtel, but now he had control over his life, and control was all that mattered.

Preston decided to start a business in the new field of dog agility. The sport went through explosive growth and his timing proved perfect. His classes were full of starstruck middle-aged women who paid $80 apiece for six group lessons. He charged $100 an hour for private lessons, and his calendar was always full. His best moneymaker, the four-day Power Control Camp, cleared $40,000 after expenses. Sales of T-shirts, sweat suits, and other gear sporting his logo brought in a nice hunk of change.

The articles he wrote for agility magazines produced only modest stipends, but they kept his name out there, and the ladies flocked to his training field: three acres in Gilroy that produced a nice tax write-off. He deducted his travel expenses and entry fees for the numerous competitions he entered.

His Aussies would run through a brick wall for him. He had owned a border collie once, but she just wasn't tough enough. He thought border collies were too soft, too temperamental. They wanted to work at a distance, they ran too fast, and they were independent thinkers. Preston preferred a dog he could control.

The Aussies constantly checked in with Preston as they ran. They had one eye on the master at all times, always under his control, turning on a dime at full speed, although sometimes too quickly, like the bitch that ripped the ACL on her right hind leg. The surgery to repair would have cost Preston $4000, but even then she would never compete again. He turned her over to an Australian shepherd rescue group. She'd make someone a nice pet.

Preston's tight little group of prized students made plans for dinner the first night, a chance to relax and rub elbows, and perhaps pick up a few tips from the master who was always in control. Preston decided to invite someone to join them, a pretty young woman who seemed to be alone. She had a border collie that appeared to be his only serious competition that weekend.

"Is this your first championship?" asked Preston.

Cassy recognized the competition leader with the wavy black hair. She smiled. "Yes, I guess I've got a lot to learn."

Preston studied her dog carefully. "How long have you had that dog?"

"My grandfather got her from an animal rescue group several months ago."

Myst cowered, tucked her tail, and peed as Preston stared at her. Cassy wasn't surprised. Her border collie behaved apprehensively with strangers, especially men. She displayed all the behavioral characteristics of physical abuse. It had taken a lot of nurturing to help Myst regain her confidence. Cassy hoped the agility competitions would help.

Preston smiled at her. "If you really want to go somewhere in this sport, you need a more confident dog. I've seen dogs like this. I've always preferred Aussies because they're tough. I've seen them kicked by cattle and hardly be fazed."

"Myst is soft, but she's my pet now. I'll make the best of it."

"Look, don't baby her. Let her know who's in charge. I can hardly hear your voice when you give commands in the ring."

"I guess you're right. It's just that I'm so nervous."

"Nervous? Maybe this'll help." Preston began massaging her neck and shoulders. She tensed, but as his strong hands kneaded her shoulders, she began to relax.

"How's that?

"Much better."

She joined Preston, Abigail, and a small group of dog handlers at dinner that night. They only knew each other superficially, so the conversations centered mostly on their dogs, their successes and failures.

"Is Ringo your only dog?" Cassy asked Preston.

"Actually, I have five Aussies and a mixed breed. I tried border collies for a while, but they didn't work out. BC's were bred to herd sheep, they like to work away from the handler, and they're harder to control. Too independent for my taste. The females, like your dog, aren't tough enough for competitions and may quit. An Aussie will stay at your side and respond immediately to commands."

Cassy had seen Myst quit. In the beginning, she would freeze in the ring if the judge got too near. She even ran out of the ring on occasion, but she also had some special qualities: lightning quick reflexes, great jumping ability, and she learned quickly. "Aren't there times when the dog needs to work away from the handler?" she said. "I mean, there's no way I can run as fast as my dog."

"That's where control comes in. Sometimes, your dog is halfway across the ring from you. No dog of mine would ever get too far away. Without my guidance, they would crash and burn."

"Crash and burn?"

Abigail put down her fork and jumped into the conversation. "Speed can be a curse. Some dogs are manic. Too fast for their own good. They flatten out on jumps and knock bars down. If a handler's timing is off by milliseconds, the dogs go off course. Speed causes dogs to get burned. My golden, Dreamer, has just the right combination of speed and control."

Preston added, "I want total control of my dogs."

"How do you train for that?" asked Cassy

"I like to use an electronic collar. If the dog gets too far away, I give it an electric shock. Only takes once or twice."

Cassy grimaced. "There's got to be a better way."

Abigail responded, "Some trainers have experimented with clicker training, but even if it works, it's a much slower process. You train the behavior you want with a toy clicker."

"Have you ever tried clicker training?" Cassy asked Preston.

"I don't have time for that nonsense."

After dinner, Preston offered to take Cassy back to her motel. Abigail and the others rode together to the Hampton Inn.

"Thanks for the ride," Cassy said, when they arrived at Motel 7. "I enjoyed dinner."

"You don't have to go in right now. Let's talk awhile."

"Maybe tomorrow. I want to check on my dog."

Preston rested his arm on the top of Cassy's seat. "You know, I really like you."

She stared at him. "Are you married?"

He dropped his arm around her shoulder. "My wife and I aren't that close. Why do you think I go to these dog shows alone?"

Cassy turned toward the door. "I have to go. I want to check on Myst."

"Dammit, forget about her. That dog will never be a winner."

Anger welled inside Cassy. "Maybe not, but we'll do the best we can."

"Believe me, that dog is a loser."

"How do you know?"

"Because I'm a dog trainer. I've seen lots of dogs."

"Dogs can be different, even dogs of the same breed."

Preston pointed his finger at her as if he were lecturing a child. "Believe me, I know border collies."

"You don't know my dog."

"Yes, I do."

"How can you say that?"

"Because I trained her at one time."

"Excuse me? Whose dog was she?"

Preston hesitated a second and slumped back again his seat. "Hell, I had that dog for a few months. She wasn't tough enough."

"So you dropped her off in a box at the animal shelter in the middle of the night?"

"Grow up. I knew she'd be adopted. I cut my losses."

"Did you shock her?"

Preston looked away. "I can't remember."

"Really? I'll bet she does. Do you know she was seconds away from being put down?"

"Thousands of dogs are euthanized. The animal shelters are full of unwanted dogs."

"You bastard." Cassy pushed his arm aside, slid out of the car, and slammed the door.

The following evening after the scores were tallied, Preston accepted the California Cup. He took the customary victory lap around the field with Ringo to the polite applause of the few who remained at that late hour. He had won for the third year in a row. A few discontented also-rans grumbled that they had to train their dogs while maintaining a full-time job. For Preston, dog agility was his day job. His reputation grew with each victory. More aspiring wannabes flocked to his business.

Abigail hugged her second-place ribbon, her fragile self-esteem saved that weekend. Her steady golden retriever beat the faster dogs by playing it safe and not making mistakes. She decided she would travel to the North American

Championships in the fall, and then who knew what might happen? Somehow, she'd find the money for classes and seminars and private lessons to keep her dreams alive.

After spending a sleepless night, Cassy had lacked focus on the last day of the competition. Her command timing in the ring with her dog had been a disaster. Somehow, it didn't matter. Questions about Myst had been answered. She felt more angry than disappointed. A fire had been ignited inside her. She needed to find the right person to take her to the next step, someone who could explain clicker training, and who wasn't a control freak.

22 Clicking

Liam made an effort to emerge from the doghouse the first weekend in May. He'd heard about the Susan Barrett Clicker Training seminar sponsored by the Bay Barkers Club. He'd learned Cassy was seeing a teacher at Sonoma State. Although he had little hope of getting her to join him, surprisingly, she told him she'd be delighted.

Saturday morning, they drove to Petaluma for the seminar. Pleased to be in her good graces again, he tried to break the ice with clever conversation. "You know, clickers were used during the Second World War."

Cassy looked straight ahead. "Yes."

Undaunted, he said, "Allied paratroopers used them in Normandy to communicate in the dark after they landed behind enemy lines."

She answered in a measured monotone. "I know that."

"I believe they're also called crickets."

She leaned back against the headrest and closed her eyes. "Right."

So maybe the ice had not completely thawed. Liam felt a little intimidated, but was impressed by her focus. He saw the clicker event as a way to enjoy a warm spring Saturday. She seemed to see it as a kind of dog-training CPR.

Each of the eight participants received a toy clicker. Promptly at nine, Susan Barrett began the first lesson. "The methods we'll use today are similar to those used to train dolphins and other animals. Sit on the floor next to your dogs. Look at them, but don't pet them and don't talk to them. When they begin any type of activity – scratching, licking their lips, touching you, barking, anything – click and give them a treat. Whatever the activity is, that's the first behavior you reinforce. Reward that behavior as often as you can in the next ten minutes."

Liam sat next to Storm and looked into his dark brown eyes. His dog leaned forward and gave his master a wet sloppy kiss on his right eye.

Susan admonished him, "Click and treat."

Liam protested, "But he didn't do anything."

"Yes, he did. He licked your face. That's the behavior you'll train."

Liam began the drill again, but Storm looked bored and lay down. He didn't repeat his sloppy kiss for the remainder of the drill.

He felt Cassy's intensity a little unnerving. She seemed to be taking this activity very seriously. Myst put her left front paw on her arm. Click, followed by a treat. Thirty seconds later, Myst repeated the behavior for another reward. At the end of ten minutes, the dog had touched Cassy's arm more than twenty times.

Susan congratulated the class. "That was excellent. I want the gentleman with the flat-coat to repeat stage one. Everyone else, add a word to prompt the same behavior. If the dog responds correctly click, treat, and say, 'Good dog.' Eventually, the treat will be replaced by verbal praise alone. In the final stage, the click will be eliminated. You may begin."

"Touch," said Cassy. Myst reached out with her left paw. Click and treat. "Good dog."

Storm appeared to take a keen interest in the nearby dogs getting food and raised his right paw. He shook it limply in the air. Click and treat.

As the morning progressed, all eight dogs quickly learned a variety of trained behaviors. The dogs were trained to sit, stay, come, and lie down. Click and treat. "Good dog."

After lunch, everyone moved outside to the lawn, where a few practice jumps were set up. New commands were taught. The dogs were taught to take a jump and come back to the handler. "Tight." Click and treat. "Good dog." Next lesson: take a jump, and then move away from the handler. "Switch." Click and treat. "Good dog." They learned to move straight ahead and take distant obstacles. "Out." Click & treat. "Good dog."

Myst already had those skills. She already worked at great distances following body motions. The only elements missing were the commands.

On their way home, Liam glanced at Cassy, who had a slight smile and appeared deep in thought. "Did you have a good time today?" he asked.

The question broke her concentration. "Yes." She hesitated. "I learned something last weekend...something about Myst."

"What's that?"

"Remember Preston Wadsworth?"

"Sure. He whistled Storm out of the ring at our first trial for running around the ring with a number cone in his mouth. Didn't seem to have a sense of humor."

"He's a scumbag."

"Whoa!"

Her eyes narrowed. "He owned Myst for a while, tried to train her by God only knows what methods. He did say he used electric collars on his dogs. Anyway, he's the creep who dumped her at the animal shelter in the middle of the night."

Liam took a deep breath. "So that's the cur."

Cassy started to giggle. "Don't insult mixed breed dogs."

"Has Frank been bothering you the past few months?"

"I heard he moved back north."

Sensing the ice thawing, Liam took a chance. "You know, I've heard the best trainer in the country has summer camps in Idaho. How'd you like to take that in? We could camp out, save a few dollars."

"Idaho? Where astronauts had walk-on-the-moon training? You want to camp on a moonscape?"

"Not Craters of the Moon National Monument. The camp is up in the panhandle. Beautiful mountains, very scenic."

"The only thing I know about Idaho is potatoes."

Liam tried another strategy. "Do you know why the Idaho potato went to the beach?"

Cassy put her hand to her chin and her eyes rolled upward. "Let me see...he wanted to get baked?"

"Old joke," said Liam.

"Yeah, good try. Is it okay for you to leave the state?"

"I'll check with my lawyer."

"Let me think some about the camping. I'll need to get Ida to stay with Ben."

"How's she working out?"

"He likes her. Says she's a good listener."

"That's good news," said Liam.

"I'd like to visit Claire in Eureka, but I don't think my old Datsun can make it that far. Would you consider—?"

"Sure. I'll drive. Sounds like fun. Then we can go to Idaho after Claire."

23 Things To Do in Humboldt County Before You're Shot

Unlike the monotonously linear Interstate 5 to the east, Highway 101 followed the gentle curves and contours of the coastal range, but far enough from the coast to miss the natural summer air conditioning. Ahead on the road, overheated air shimmered above the asphalt. The van's temperature gauge rose perilously as they negotiated the long uphill stretches, so Liam turned off the car's air conditioning. He was glad the dogs were staying with Ben and didn't have to deal with the heat.

"Turn it back on!" Cassy wailed and rolled down her window. Thunderous road noise accompanied a blast of superheated air that blew inside.

"The engine's overheating. Wait until we reach the crest of this hill." Liam glanced over at her auburn hair blowing in the wind. Her face looked more youthful than her thirty-something years. Hell, he was past forty. Maybe he was too old for her. He'd only known her a few months. What had he gotten himself into?

After cresting the long incline, they rolled up the windows, and Liam turned the air back on. The road noise subsided to a more comfortable level.

"How far are we from Willits?" asked Cassy.

"About ten miles. Doesn't Willits have an old steam train that travels from Willits to Fort Bragg through the redwoods?"

"Yeah, the Skunk train. You can smell it before you can see it." Cassy rolled her eyes. "Willits's a real wide-open town. Sometimes, people stay up past nine o'clock."

"Did you and Claire ever spend time there?"

"As little as possible."

Liam looked to his left. "Hey, a sign for the Black Bart Casino. Poker slots."

"Yeah, I think it's new. For real excitement, Claire and I went to Buster's Bar and Grill a couple times."

"How was it?"

"A dump. I hoped no one would recognize me."

"Why?"

She looked a little sheepish. "I was supposed to be living in a tree."

"Wait a minute! You'd wave at the TV cameras during the day, and at night you'd go to Buster's Bar and Grill?"

"Well, the Skunk train didn't run at night. I was going out of my mind. We finally had to quit going to Buster's, though."

"Why?"

"Because the unemployed loggers were beating the crap out of anyone who smelled like an environmentalist."

Liam smiled. "After a month in that tree, I'll bet you smelled like an environmentalist."

"They were even tougher on anyone who threatened their second source of income – growing pot."

"What did they do?"

"They shot 'em."

"You're kidding."

Cassy smiled slyly as she looked at him out of the corner of her green eyes. She had a devilish streak that could be unsettling, or enticing, or both. "Well, not all of them."

Early that afternoon they entered Humboldt County. The road narrowed to two lanes and snaked between magnificent redwoods, presenting occasional views of the South Fork of the Eel River. At a place called French's Camp, the most incredible sight unfolded down by the river: a vast campground of tents and vehicles. Bare-chested young men, many with long hair in dreadlocks, and girls in halter-tops and shorts were everywhere.

"Oh, my God! It's Reggae on the River!" said Cassy.

"Where people sit around beating on steel kettles?"

"Not always. These concerts began years ago, and I've never been to one. Pull over."

Liam tried to park along the road, but a traffic cop motioned him to keep moving. He rolled down his window to ask directions. "Where can I park?"

"Benbow Lake Campground," yelled the cop. "Take the shuttle back."

They parked at the campground in time to see the shuttle arrive with a small group of Reggae fans leaving for the day, including two glassy-eyed teenagers. The taller youngster's face was sunburned beet red because he wore his hat in rally cap position. His shirtless companion wore a black broad-brimmed hat and baggy shorts that slipped so low he probably didn't need to wear them at all.

"How's the music?" asked Cassy.

Rally Cap stopped puffing on a funny-looking cigarette. "Diggedy dank, dudes. It's peace and love and stuff."

"Yeah, it has a good beat and everything," added the zombie in the black hat, who stared off into space and didn't seem to be talking to anyone in particular.

"Do you guys have extra tickets?" Cassy asked.

"Naw. Sold out. We would have stayed longer, but we ran out of weed," said Rally Cap, who stared at Cassy with his mouth open. He turned to Liam. "This is our last one. Want a hit, man?"

"Thanks, but—"

"Yeah, thanks," interrupted Cassy. She took the joint between her thumb and forefinger, tilted her head back dramatically, took a long slow drag and held it until Liam feared she might pass out. She exhaled with considerable flair. "Here, go ahead, Liam."

He looked around nervously and returned the joint to Rally Cap. "Sorry. Trying to cut back."

"So, are you guys leaving?" Cassy asked. She smiled, put her hands on her hips, and shifted her weight backward seductively.

"Yeah, you want our bracelets?"

"Oh, thanks, you guys are so cool," she cooed.

The bracelets were plastic strips that showed the bearers had tickets and were free to come and go to the concert. Liam cut the bracelets from the teens' wrists and found some super glue in the glove compartment to reconnect them. The counterfeiters were in business.

Cassy put on black shorts and a tie-dyed T-shirt with a picture of Janis Joplin. She carried a beach towel. Liam selected a black T-shirt from his duffel bag, a gift from a pal at

Berkeley. The front showed a pair of bird wings and lightning bolts over the Genentech logo, with the slogan "Clone or Die" centered above. Liam wasn't quite sure how asexual reproduction related to mortality, but this slogan sounded bad. He stuffed a $20 bill in his shorts, locked his wallet in the glove compartment, and laced the van key to his running shoes.

Cassy stared at her traveling companion. "What are you doing?"

"I don't have to worry about losing my wallet or keys this way." He sprayed his legs with Cutter's. "Mosquitoes. You know, the West Nile virus."

"Loosen up! Oh, God. I'll take my chances. Promise me you'll be a free spirit today."

"I'll be the reincarnation of Jack Kerouac."

"Who?"

"Kerouac, a beat generation writer. Fifties."

"You mean like Allen Ginsberg, Burroughs, or Corso?"

"You're messing with me again."

"Lighten up, Kerouac. Remember, my grandmother was an English teacher, and we didn't just grow rutabagas in New Mexico."

They caught the next shuttle back to the event. After flashing their bracelets at a security checkpoint, they started the hike down to the Eel River.

Tents, cars, RV's, and nearly 10,000 people sprawled as far as the eye could see. The rhythmic sounds of reggae filled the air. Those near the stage danced and swayed to the slow drawl of the metallic calypso rhythm. The garb ranged from string bikinis to full-length African caftans. Some wore nothing but their TEVA sandals. Farther north from the stage, small groups splashed in the shallow river water. Liam bought a couple of hot dogs and two bottles of Humboldt Pale Ale. After eating, they walked through the campground to the river.

Keeping their running shoes on, they waded into the shallow water and walked along the gravel base. The cool water was delightfully sensuous compared to an air temperature still in the upper nineties. The rapidly moving current massaged their feet. Their hands slid together.

They walked around a bend in the river until they were alone. Liam nervously offered geological information. "Fast-moving water is invariably shallow like this."

"Mom used to say that still water runs deep." She looked straight into his eyes, started laughing, and ran through the water, holding the beach towel over her head like a fluttering flag. She stopped, removed her tie-dyed shirt, and tossed it toward the bank. She ran braless through the shallow water, squealing, and holding the flapping towel over her head with both hands. Liam looked around nervously. He tossed his T-shirt and raced after her, unleashing his best primal scream.

He caught up after fifty yards. She must have wanted to be caught because she didn't seem to be breathing as hard as he was. They were both suddenly silent. She took his hand. They walked to a shady spot on the riverbank and laid her towel on the ground.

My lucky day, thought Liam. *Better than poker slots at the Black Bart Casino.*

The sun had dipped low in the northwest when they headed back towards the campground, wrapped together in the beach towel. Liam wasn't concerned at first when he failed to find his T-shirt, but after ten minutes, it became clear their shirts were gone.

"Why would someone take my T-shirt?" he asked.

Cassy lifted her face to the sky and mockingly replied, "Are you serious? That would've been the first thing I'd grab." She rubbed her arm.

"Are you scratching?"

"Yeah, I think I got some mosquito bites."

Darkness had set in before they reached the highway. The temperature dropped dramatically. They boarded the nearly empty shuttle and moved to the back as unobtrusively as possible. They shared the beach towel and huddled together for warmth. An elderly couple four seats away gave them a disapproving look and moved to the front of the bus.

As the bus headed back to the campground, the sounds of reggae drifted up from the canyon and gradually faded away. Cassy poked Liam in the ribs with her elbow. "Well, Kerouac, did you have a good time today?"

They were on the Redwood Highway again at 8:30 that night. Near the coast, fog replaced the inland heat, and the temperature dropped into the low fifties. Shortly before ten, they entered Eureka.

Cassy woke from a mini-nap. "Turn right past the shopping center. 2432 Harris Street."

Liam strained to read street signs through billows of thick fog drifting in from the ocean. After turning onto Harris Street, they drove through a dreary old business area, then past the fairgrounds and some small, rundown houses. Three miles from the Redwood Highway the neighborhood began to look more upscale. They located a well-kept salmon-colored Victorian two-story with a porch light on and parked on a crescent-shaped driveway. A silver-colored

Lexus sat outside the attached garage. Their headlights faintly illuminated a solitary figure in the window.

"It's Claire." Cassy bolted from the van.

Claire opened the front door. "Ohmygod!"

The two women embraced, shrieking, and carrying on so that Liam expected the neighbors to start complaining.

"This is Liam," Cassy said.

Claire Delfano looked to be Cassy's age, but taller and a little heavier. She wore jeans and a sleeveless white blouse and had a rose tattoo on her left shoulder. "I've heard so much about you," she said to Liam. "Nice to meet you. Let's go inside. Can I get you something?"

Liam nursed a Humboldt pale ale. He watched Cassy and Claire chatter away. Cassy had said Claire worked as a waitress, so how could she afford to live in a quaint Victorian with a Lexus in the driveway?

"I've been living with Tony the past six months, " Claire said. "If he pops the question, I want you to be maid of honor."

"Oh, of course. I'm so happy for you."

"What does Tony do?" Liam asked.

"He was a logger until he got laid off. He's in agriculture now."

Cassy looked surprised. "He's a farmer?"

"I guess you could say that."

"You mean he grows pot?"

"Don't look so shocked. You know how tough it is to get by up here."

"I hope you know what you're getting into."

Claire seemed unperturbed. "Tony and the other growers have an unspoken agreement with the ATF. Once every three years, the fields get raided. He gets tipped off, so he's never there. The Feds take lots of photos and get a nice spot on TV. Everyone knows they're just pissing in the wind. The new crop is planted on federal land minutes after the old crop is hauled away."

Cassy looked skeptical. "Business must be good."

"So far, so good. The only guys not cooperating are Frank's buddies. They're greedy SOBs. They're trying to crowd out everyone else. I guess I really shouldn't say too much. I'm afraid I've said too much already. Hey, are you guys hungry?"

"I'm starving. How about you, Liam?"

"I saw a Pizza Hut in the shopping center on the way in. I can pick up something."

"I'm expecting Tony home soon," Claire said. "He'll be hungry. The pizza place closes at 11:30."

"Tell me what you want," Liam said.

"I'll come with you," Cassy said.

The porch light reflected dimly off the thick coastal fog that was rapidly turning to a drizzle. The only sounds came from a distant foghorn. Liam started the van and turned on the lights. Glancing in the rearview mirror, he saw two vehicles on the street behind them turn on their headlights. He turned on the windshield wipers and drove into the street. The two vehicles followed. After one block, the lead vehicle quickly passed. The large black truck made a sudden 180-degree turn and stopped, blocking the street. A second vehicle pulled in behind, blocking their movement forward and backward.

Cassy, ashen-faced, took a deep breath.

Liam's heart pounded. In the rear-view mirror, he watched the driver of the truck emerge carrying a rifle in one hand slung low on his right side. Liam turned to Cassy.

"I believe we're about to meet the Eureka welcoming committee. Stay here. Lock the doors. Don't look at their faces. I don't think they want to talk to you…I love you."

He got out with his hands in the air to make it clear he was unarmed. His legs shaking, he walked forward and faced the large dark figure with the rifle silhouetted by the lights of his truck.

The shadowy figure tipped the rifle up slightly and stopped twenty feet away. "Who are you? Are you friends with that weasel, Frank?"

A door opened and closed behind Liam. The windshield wipers on his van continued to drag and whoosh in rhythm, matching his beating heart in an offbeat Reggae time. He feared his voice would crack, but surprisingly it was steady and low-pitched. "My name is Liam Gallagher. The girl in the car is not looking at you. Please leave her alone. If this is about Frank, I want you to know he's a son-of-a-bitch. He tries to push old men and women around, and he slinks around at night like a slime fungus."

The gunman advanced. Liam glanced to his left and saw Cassy walking toward him. She took his left hand. The mysterious figure lowered his rifle. "You're Cassy O'Neil, aren't you?"

She nodded.

"I'm Tony Martini. We saw your van parked at my house and thought you might be friends of that bastard, Frank." He moved forward and shook Liam's cold clammy right hand. "So you're the guy he framed."

Cassy whispered in Liam's ear, "I love you, too."

24 Camp Life

Mile after monotonous mile of sagebrush decorated the high desert along Highway 395 in Eastern Washington. Now and then, circles of green appeared on the landscape, as if created by aliens. Along the radius of each circle an aluminum sprinkler system, anchored in the center, slowly rotated.

As the miles passed, Liam's pending court appearance faded proportionally. The charges had been reduced to misdemeanors, and Myra's bail money had been returned. Claire heard that Frank had returned to Humboldt County, although no one had seen him there recently.

The sweltering June heat created mirror images on the superheated freeway. Cassy turned the air conditioning up a notch. "Look at that license plate. Washington, The Evergreen State. I haven't seen anything evergreen since we left Oregon."

Liam glanced at the dreary scenery. "The western half of the state gets most of the rain. This area uses irrigation water. There are fourteen dams on the Columbia River."

Cassy frowned. "And the salmon runs are near extinction because the dams block migration patterns."

"That's true, but the dams produce hydroelectric power."

"Yeah, power to produce plutonium."
Liam was sympathetic to her environmental passions, but thought she needed to lighten up. "That was at Hanford during the war. I don't think that town exists anymore."

Attracted by gas costing less than a dollar per gallon, they stopped in Pasco. While Liam filled the tank, Cassy walked the dogs.

A farmer filling up his truck looked them over. "Nice rig you've got there. Where ya headed?"

Liam replied absently. "Idaho. Must be a hundred degrees here today."

"I see you're from California. You're not one of those Sierra Club nuts, are you?"

Liam thought the comment rude, but answered politely. "We're from the Bay Area."

"Going fishing or hunting?"

"Neither. We plan to do dog training."

"You don't say. Well, I train my own dogs. Environmentalists! I can barely make ends meet and some government SOB wants to cut off my water to save freaking fish."

Not caring to get further involved in that conversation, Liam bid the farmer a good day, finished filling up, and they hit the road again.

As they pulled away, Cassy turned to Liam. "I overheard you talking to that farmer. How can you let people go on like that? Get in their face a little. The government keeps giving away cheap water and can't see the bigger picture. Sometimes, you are such a wuss."

Liam clenched his teeth, gripped the steering wheel a little tighter, and said nothing.

⌣

After entering the Northern Idaho Panhandle, they drove past a magnificent, dark blue lake at Coeur d'Alene. More breathtaking mountain scenery climaxed in the Fourth of July Pass. They took the Rose Lake exit and headed south on Highway 3. After ten miles, they turned onto a gravel road and several bumpy minutes later arrived at Sharon Nelson's dog training facility. They continued across an earthen dam that supported abandoned railroad tracks. Liam knew that at one time trains had hauled silver ore from nearby Kellogg to Spokane.

Water surrounded the sprawling campsite on three sides. Campers pitched their tents in shady sites near the water, or chose sunny meadows to avoid mosquitoes. The occasional mooing of cattle drifted across a river canal to the north. A large pond with marsh grasses marked the south perimeter. Ducks, herons, and osprey worked the rich water.

Many considered Sharon Nelson, a former computer programmer, the training guru of dog agility. Disenchanted by the established dog agility organization, she started her own: the North American Dog Agility Counsel, or NADAC. Within a few years, it became the largest dog agility venue in the world. She considered changing the acronym when she kept getting e-mail directed to the National Association of Drunks and Carousers. Her husband, Dave Nelson, ran the ranch, but somehow found time to be the camp cook. Fun-loving campers nailed a plaque to his outdoor kitchen, naming it the Road Kill Cafe.

After setting up their tent, Liam walked over to the outdoor shower. Two adjacent stalls, fashioned from rough-cut redwood planks, were joined together like a townhouse. The stalls were lined with indoor-outdoor carpeting on the floor and walls to provide privacy. Water pumped from the river filled a monstrous 550-gallon plastic storage tank perched on the roof. A hot water heater sat next to the monolith, and PVC pipe snaked to the showerhead risers.

The river had a no-wake zone. An occasional motorboat or jet skier idled past, no louder than the hum of the generator that supplied power to the shower water pump. To the west were portable toilets, carrying the incongruous name of Honey Buckets. Fortunately, a slight breeze carried the smell away from the showers.

An elderly camper joined Liam and introduced himself as Simon. "A year ago, the shower walls were tarps. Quite an engineering masterpiece, isn't it?"

"Nice to meet you," Liam said. "We're from California."

Simon wore a NADAC T-shirt and tan shorts with suspenders. "Emily and I are, as well – Northridge. After the earthquake, we used the insurance money to buy that RV." Simon pointed to a green and white motor home parked nearby.

"Very nice. I'm afraid we'll be roughing it in a tent. We've been on the road all day. Does this thing work? Is there hot water?"

"All the water in the system operates off a single inlet pipe. If you shower alone, use the left stall. It controls the water for both sides. You'll find a small railroad tie on the floor for someone too short to reach the faucets. The soapy water doesn't drain well through the carpeting and puddles. Standing on the railroad tie, you can avoid standing ankle deep in your wash water. With a partner, you have to work together. The right side siphons water from the left."

"Thanks. I'll get my girlfriend, and we'll give it a try."

"One other thing," admonished Simon. "Be careful. The hot and cold water faucets are reversed on the right side."

Liam waited barefoot at the shower, wearing only his running shorts and holding a bar of soap, a towel draped over one shoulder. Cassy approached in sandals, wearing a long white bathrobe. She carried a large bag and a towel that may have been visible from space.

Liam peeked into the bag. A quick inventory revealed washcloths, assorted bottles containing cucumber and melon extracts, a pumice stone, and various assorted items he couldn't identify. "What's all this?"

She gave him a dirty look. "Never mind."

Liam took a position on the right side and waited patiently for her to get the proper mix of hot and cold water in the master stall on the left. Every now and then, she squealed, "Too hot! Too cold!" Finally, she achieved the correct temperature, and Liam prepared to siphon water from the master stall.

"Is your cold water on the right or the left?" said Liam.

"The right."

"Here goes!" he opened the valve on the right, but to his surprise he got hot water. At that exact instant, he became aware of howling from the master stall.

"My water's cold. You did that on purpose!"

"No. I'm sorry." Liam quickly closed the hot water valve. "I think the valves are different on my side. My cold water is on the left. Let me try again."

He opened the left valve and again heard screaming that reminded him of the shower scene in the Hitchcock movie Psycho.

"Turn it off! Turn it off!"

"What happened?"

"You just about scalded me to death."

Liam quickly turned off the left valve. "I think we need to do this in stages so the temperature won't have sudden changes. "

They proceeded to do a hot water, cold-water dance in increments until both had an ideal temperature, but the water pressure for two dropped to half of the pressure for one and kept dropping. The water flow became a trickle and required continual adjustment.

After a few minutes Liam, stood ankle deep in dirty soapy water. "I need to turn off my water."

"No. Wait."

"The water's not draining on my side. Let's turn off the water together. I'll turn off the hot first, and you can adjust your cold – I mean hot." He mistakenly shut the valve on the left and they both jumped back, shrieking, as a blast of hot water attacked them. The next try was successful. After a few tries, they started to get the hang of it with a minimum of thermal torment.

"Cassy, are you done?"

"Not yet, shampooing again."

"You shampoo twice? Let me know when to turn the water back on."

"Okay, but I still have to use the conditioner."

Liam rinsed the soap scum off his feet and ankles and wrapped a towel around his waist before exiting barefoot into the dirt. She emerged in a robe with a towel on her head and put on her sandals.

Liam sniffed the air. "Your hair smells nice. That wasn't so bad, was it?"

She rolled her eyes. "I'm considering getting a new shower partner."

The next morning, campers assembled for breakfast at the Road Kill Cafe, a small shack kitchen powered by propane. Two outdoor picnic tables served the dozen campers. Chef Dave Nelson wore boots and a cowboy hat while attending to bacon and sausage frying on a large griddle. A portable tape player inside the shack played bluegrass music. Roused by the clean mountain air, birds singing, and mosquitoes whining, everyone had developed Paul Bunyanesque appetites. They munched on fruit and opened little boxes of cereal set out for pre-breakfast snacking. Liam had two.

They got in line behind the other campers, and in a few minutes stood before the chef.

"How do you like your eggs?"

"Scrambled, please."

Dave proceeded to prepare a culinary masterpiece that included cheese, onions, and ham. When finished, he heaped generous portions of the omelet onto both their plates. "Bacon?"

"Sure."

"Sausage?"

Liam's appetite had only been partly satiated by the cereal, so he took three sausages. Cassy asked for one.

"How many pancakes?" Dave motioned to Frisbee-sized portions.

Cassy's eyes got as big as saucers. "Looks awfully inviting, but I'll have to pass. I don't see how I can eat all this."

Liam didn't want to sound unappreciative. "I'll take two."

They joined a table with Simon, his wife, Emily, and four others.

"Is this your first camp?" asked Emily.

"Yes," Cassy replied. "Have you been here before?"

"This is our third summer. Simon decided to try his hand at judging after the first year. He completed his training last summer."

Cassy replied between mouthfuls. "I admire how hard the judges work at the trials – on their feet all day in the sun, or cold, or whatever." She watched Liam struggling to finish his breakfast. "You don't have to finish that."

"My mother insisted I finish my meals, something about starving Armenians. If you didn't clean your plate, you contributed to someone in the world going hungry."

Cassy evidently had no guilt about starving people and didn't finish her sausage.

After breakfast, Liam loosened his belt two notches, and went back to the van to get a hammer and screwdriver. He walked past the Honey Buckets to the shower and poked holes in the carpeting where the water had collected the day before.

The morning and afternoon were spent training with Sharon. Myst learned each new drill quickly and had a marvelous day, except when she rolled on a dead fish. After each drill, Storm ran from the field and dove into the river. Later that afternoon, Cassy took the dogs swimming to clean up.

Liam walked to the shower and prepared for a solo experience. He tried to set the optimum water temperature, but there was no hot water. He was amazed at how cold the water felt in contrast to an air temperature of 90°, but he shampooed, soaped up, and rinsed. By the time he was finished, he again stood ankle deep in dirty, soapy water. The holes he'd punched into the carpeting had filled like punctures in a self-sealing tire.

He headed back to the tent, slightly annoyed that the wind had shifted and was now gusting from the direction of the Honey Buckets.

25 The Whole Stinking Story

The night sky brightened as if lit up by a giant flash bulb. Within a second, thunder reverberated in the mountain valley. A torrent of rain and a barrage of hail shelled the tent. After ten minutes, it stopped suddenly, and the occupants nervously awaited an encore.

Cassy turned on a flashlight. "Water's coming in. I'm moving to the van."

Liam agreed. "Good idea."

They took advantage of the lull in the rain to move the dogs, sleeping bags, and whatever else they could quickly relocate, finishing in the nick of time. The rain returned and pelted the van for the rest of the night.

Shortly after sunrise, Liam dumped a few gallons of water from their tent. Fortunately, the only belongings they'd left behind were towels and bathing suits, which Liam hung on bushes to dry. Pools of water dotted the saturated campground.

Simon left his Winnebago and walked over. "I was worried about you guys. Looked out the window last night and saw you transferring to the van. Everything okay?"

"Thanks, we're fine. How about yourselves?"

"My only worry is driving out tomorrow. The ground's pretty soft. We almost got stuck driving in, and that was before the storm last night. Sam Goldman tried to leave early this morning and got bogged down. He called a tow truck. Only one place answered his call, and they wanted cash."

"Are you driving straight home at the end of camp?" Liam asked.

"No. There's a trial in Calgary next weekend. About an eight-hour drive. If you're interested, it's not too late to enter. It's a pretty drive up route 95 through Bonner's Ferry into Alberta."

"I heard about trouble at Ruby Ridge a couple years ago."

Simon nodded. "The Federal Government believed it was a stronghold for a group of white supremacists. U.S. Marshals raided a cabin belonging to Randy Weaver in 1992. His wife and son were killed in a firefight."

"I heard there might be neo-Nazi groups in that area."

"Supposedly. Aryan Nations has a compound near Hayden Lake. They've had rallies in Coeur d'Alene."

Later that morning, a large black tow truck arrived. It looked like one of those monster trucks that chase teenagers in horror movies. It had a pair of gigantic searchlights, oversized tires, and a massive bumper that could have been recycled from a tank.

Liam spotted a six-pack of ale on the passenger seat. The driver looked annoyed, and his frown matched the curvature of his shaved head. His black leather vest hung open over a dirty T-shirt. He turned his head and spit a wad of tobacco juice, wiping his day-old stubble. He walked haltingly over to Sam Goldman.

"I'm Marty. That'll be three Andrew Jacksons."

Sam fumbled through his wallet for three twenties. "Should we remove the dogs before you pull us out?"

"I don't give a crap. I'll be back in a minute."

Simon turned to Liam. "Did you see the swastika between his thumb and forefinger?"

Marty backed his truck into position and retrieved a pair of chains from the flatbed of his black colossus. He glanced at the California license plates on Liam's van and mumbled, "Next it'll be the pinheads from the sunshine state. Who the hell teaches you guys to drive?"

Liam shot back, "Actually, I think the sunshine state is Florida."

"Listen, smart ass, you want that guy's RV out of the mud or not? You know, I hear the last earthquake shook all the fruits and nuts into California." He turned to Sam. "Get in and start the engine. Put it in neutral and steer a straight line. Think you can remember that?"

Sam did his best to answer politely. "I'll try."

Marty had Sam's RV out of the mud in a jiffy. He spit a wad of tobacco juice and left.

Sam said goodbye to everyone and added, "You know, I've lived in Spokane for the last thirty years. Believe me. The people up here wish this lunatic fringe would disappear."

"Yeah," said Simon. "That guy seemed about as sharp as a bowling ball."

Later that afternoon, Betty, the Porta-Potty lady, arrived to great rejoicing. A week of camping had left the current fleet of structures sadly overtaxed. Two new units balanced precariously on the flatbed behind her cab. She drove cautiously past the row of latrines, positioning her truck to siphon waste into a holding tank. Her front wheels began to sink alarmingly in the soft earth. Soon, she found herself in the same predicament that had befallen Sam.

Betty, a robust woman with a crew cut, stepped gingerly out of the cab to survey the situation. The new units on the truck bed rocked from side to side. "Damn. Can you guys help? I need a push."

Liam viewed the tottering Porta-Potties. He hesitated before answering. "I don't think we've got enough muscle. I'm afraid you need to call for help."

Thirty minutes later, Marty returned, his gait more unsteady than before. A score of campers gathered to watch the drama unfold.

"I'm so pleased you're here," Betty said. "Can I help?"

"Stay away from me, fruitcake," Marty warned.

Marty operated on automatic pilot. He chained his black behemoth to Betty's truck and pulled it out of the mud in no time. The new units, supported by chains, wavered precariously. Then a new problem developed. Marty's truck sunk slowly near the older units that needed cleaning. He gunned his engine, spinning the rear wheels furiously, but to no avail.

"Son of a bitch," Marty bellowed.

"Oh, what a shame," Betty deadpanned.

Despite his impaired condition, Marty had a plan. "Look, lady, we're still chained together. Cut your wheels to the left and pull forward."

Betty followed instructions and drove forward, pulling the tow truck out of the mud a few yards past the camp units. It appeared everyone had clear sailing. Marty unchained the vehicles, nervously eying the teetering structures on the back of Betty's flatbed.

Marty marched back to his truck. "I've never seen such a sorry ass bunch of losers." He raced the engine, but in his haste he had it in reverse gear instead of drive. He slammed into the camp Porta-Potties at a frightening speed, producing a very smelly explosion.

"Son of a bitch," he screamed, as he jumped out. He landed in a pool of bluish liquid floating on other materials that defied description. He tottered, trying desperately not to fall and flailing frantically until he splashed down.

"Anyone who laughs is in deep crap," Marty yelled.

"No," Liam called out. "That clearly is your territory."

"I'm going to remember this."

Liam suppressed a laugh. "I'd be surprised if you didn't."

Cassy looked at Liam and held up her right hand. Liam completed the high five with his left.

Marty cocked his fists and lunged at Liam, but slipped again and fell forward, creating another blue splash. He got to his feet with some difficulty and left immediately. It took an hour for Betty to clean up the mess with a vacuum hose. Simon and Liam took turns washing down the area with a hose used to pump river water to the showers. Occasionally, one would start to snicker, and soon they were both convulsing with laughter.

That night, Cassy and Liam sat outside the tent, stargazing. "What's that bright star overhead?" she asked.

"Well, see the Big Dipper? Follow the arc of the handle to that star. It's called Arcturus." He looked at her out of the corner of his eyes. "Do you really think I'm a wuss?"

She smiled. "After today? No. Hey, come here so I can give you a hug."

26 Exit at Weave Pole Ten

Run naked. It's a rule for the dog, not for the handler. A dog can't wear a collar in competition. It might catch on a piece of equipment and hang the pet. Furthermore, handlers can't take food or toys into the ring to bribe their teammate. Finally, handlers can't touch their dog during the test.

The hardest skill for dogs to master is learning to do the weave poles correctly. Twelve black and white poles are positioned twenty inches apart in a straight line. The dog enters from the right side, between poles one and two, and zigzags through the line of poles like a slalom skier. A memorable execution sounds like a small boy dragging a stick along a picket fence until the dog exits on the left side. "Clack, clack, clack." Remarkable dogs, like sleek border collies, their noses low to the ground, could do this in a shade over two seconds. No matter how many mistakes these dogs made in other parts of the course, when they exited the weave poles, crowds went crazy in adulation.

Liam had one unfulfilled fantasy…well, maybe more than one. Someday, he'd like to have a dog that could do the weave poles so fast that the crowd would gasp in awe.

One of the most remarkable dogs Liam had ever seen was Tess, a border collie trained by a cantankerous old man from

Calgary, Alberta. Angus McDonnell, one of the participants in the Idaho camp, was tall and lean with a white beard and hawk-like features. He wore tweed knee breeches, a matching vest, and a checkered cap. His comely sheepdog could always be found at his feet when not training. The other campers called him The Shepherd, and avoided him because he always seemed to be in a bad mood. No one questioned his dog training abilities.

During a break in the seminar, Liam timidly approached The Shepherd. "Hi, Angus. I'm training my flat-coated retriever."

"Ah've been watchin' ye."

"How did you train Tess to weave so fast?"

"Weren't as hard as the nitwits here are goin' on about."

"I've tried using wires to guide my dog through the poles properly."

"Aye, 'at's why yer dog is so bloody awful."

Undaunted, Liam pressed on. "What did you do?"

"Ah think ye might be able to understand if'n I show ye."

Angus walked over to twelve weave poles in a straight line and moved the second, fourth, and every other even pole six inches to the right. The repositioned poles now formed a narrow alley. "Poles!" he commanded quietly.

Tess immediately jumped up and raced through the poles so fast that, if you blinked, you'd miss it. Next, Angus moved the poles on the right three inches closer to those on the left, narrowing the alley. Once again, Tess was a black and white blur as she executed her weaving talent. Finally, the poles were arranged in a straight line. "Poles!"

"Clack, clack, clack." With no drop in speed, the border collie, nose down, plowed through twelve poles, lightly clipping each one with the sides of her body.

"Ah think even ye can figure out what to do noo."

"Can I try this?"

"Aye."

Liam repeated the drills Tess had performed, except he held a slice of hot dog in front of his dog to encourage him.

"Pat, pat, pat." Storm carefully avoided each pole with his eyes firmly on the hot dog slice.

"How's that, Angus?"

"Are you for real? 'At's a bonny dug, but he needs someone who knows hoo tae train 'im."

Liam's confidence took a hit. "What did I do wrong?"

"First, eat the hot dug. Ye musn't take food inta the ring or ya get the bloody boot."

In past competitions, Storm had appeared to knock the poles out of the way. He ripped his 70-pound body through the poles with such frenzy that he occasionally skipped a few. His immense size by agility standards was a distinct handicap. His big body and tail had contorted like an arthritic reptile that couldn't bend fast enough. Nevertheless, the sight of the big dog slamming away often brought nods of approval from spectators.

"Do you mind if I try again?"

"Do as ye like."

Liam tried a different motivational strategy. After completing the drills, he tossed a tennis ball past the poles. Clearly energized, Storm retrieved the ball, ran across the meadow, and launched himself into the river.

By the time Liam pulled him from the river, Angus had disappeared, which may have been just as well. Liam didn't expect to get positive feedback.

As Liam and Cassy prepared to leave camp on their way to Canada, Angus walked toward the van.

"Aye, 'e's a bugger."

"Storm?"

"Aye," replied Angus. "The black dug's not swift and won't learn quickly. Ye and 'e are a good match. Ye must learn th' rules. Ye musn't have a ball in the ring."

"I thought it would help in his training."

"Ye musn't tooch the dug as well."

"But I've heard if a trial run is going poorly, a handler is allowed to say, 'May we be excused?' pick up the dog, and leave the ring."

"Oh mon, you're not listenin'. Ye need tae learn th' rules. Just remember what ah taught ye."

"Thanks, I will."

After a scenic ride from Idaho, Liam and Cassy entered their dogs in the Provincial Championships in Calgary. The Spruce Meadows Equestrian Center hosted the event. It promised to be an event well suited for Storm, who thrived on crowds and noise.

Most of the time, Storm appeared fearless. The only time he had seemed alarmed was when he spotted a pile of clothes on the floor of Liam's dimly lit cottage. He stopped. His tail rose. He uttered in his deepest bass voice, "Woof." The phantom creature remained stationary.

Cassy asked Liam, "Did you hang up your clothes?"

"No. I think my dog is nearsighted."

More than two hundred dogs had entered the competition being held on the Equestrian Field at Spruce Meadows. The thin prairie fog lifted before nine o'clock, and soon the air temperature had climbed to a pleasant 70°. Acres of freshly cut grass produced an appealing montage with the blue skies and colorful agility equipment. The entries included Angus

McDonnell and Tess. Liam secretly hoped to show him how far he'd come since camp.

Unlike the newer lightweight agility equipment made of fiberglass and metal, the ponderous paraphernalia at this event was made of wood. It was like entering the Olympic pole vault competition and using a bamboo pole after training on a fiberglass pole. In the early rounds, dog after dog ran onto the hefty seesaw expecting it to quickly tip and, when it didn't, were launched airborne, bringing to mind the great Olympic diver, Greg Louganis. The terrifying image of a wild-eyed Pomeranian floating through the air in slow motion, with all four legs kicking, before returning mercifully to earth sent shudders through the crowd.

As Liam walked a qualifying course, he saw Angus kneeling on the ground by the weave poles. They had stripes of yellow and dark blue instead of the customary black and white.

"What do you think, Angus?"

"This is bloody awful."

"What's that?"

"Get down, ah'll show ye."

"On the ground?"

"Aye."

Liam felt a little self-conscious kneeling on the ground amid the other competitors, who were walking and learning the course, but he was curious to see what Angus had discovered.

"It's what the dug sees."

"What's that?"

Angus pointed a bony finger at the weave poles. "The yella."

"Pardon?"

"The yella and the grass."

Liam moved slightly to his left to allow a group of walkers to pass. "I think I see what you mean. The yellow and the grass blend together."

"There will be many a dug that misses the entry here. They can no' see color."

"Excuse me," Liam apologized to the woman who tripped over him.

"An' the blue. It's bloody foul."

"Yes, the blue blends in with the nearby seats. What should we do?"

"You should get out of the way," complained the exasperated woman standing over them.

"Sorry," Liam replied. "Angus, aren't the poles supposed to be white and black?"

"There's no rule. Ye should know the rules." He got up and left the ring mumbling to himself.

The qualifying runs that followed proved Angus right. Many dogs missed the entry to the weaves, including Tess.

A sizable crowd gave each team a nice round of applause as they finished, even if they screwed up. Storm could hardly wait to get in the ring. Every time the crowd applauded, he perked up.

When their turn came, Liam moved cautiously toward obstacle number one. He turned to call his dog when he caught sight of a black blur moving past him. Storm's premature start momentarily froze him, but he recovered quickly enough to get his dog through a tricky opening sequence of jumps. He signaled with his left arm and commanded, "Poles!"

Storm had a perfect entry and sliced through the weave poles like they were butter. "Clack, clack, clack." Admiring sounds came cascading down from the stands. This promised to be a memorable run. Eight, nine, ten. Only two poles remained. Storm came shooting out ready for his next challenge. He'd missed the last two poles...five faults. Qualifying for the finals became marginal.

Liam started his dog again in the poles. Eight, nine, ten... and out. The retriever looked at his handler with his proudest expression as if to say, "I'm so good today. What's next?"

It suddenly hit Liam. His nearsighted retriever didn't see those last two poles. They blended with the background. The judge held up her hand again, five faults. That did it. They had no chance to qualify. He started Storm a third time in the poles. Eight, nine, ten. As the dog rounded the tenth pole Liam gave him a slight push back into the correct position. The crowd gasped and then became stone silent. A voice boomed down from the bleachers, "Ye musn't tooch the dug!" Again the judge's arm went up, bug-eyed in disbelief.

Liam's faux pas caused him to freeze, but Storm continued on at high speed and took an A-frame trap instead of a tunnel...off course...ten faults. Liam became completely unglued. "May we be excused, please?"

The judge nodded her head in the affirmative, perhaps too shocked to answer verbally.

Storm was much too large to pick up and carry out, so Liam called him and hurried for the exit, but his dog wasn't done. He raced up the dog walk, stopped in the middle, looked around, and admired the scenery. Liam ran over and guided the flat-coat down, who stopped perfectly in the yellow safety zone. Clearly pleased with himself, the panting retriever looked left, then right, at the giggling crowd. Liam heard a whistle. The judge waved her arms, signaling for them to leave the ring

Meanwhile, Storm took off running, accompanied by increasing laughter from the crowd. Jump, jump, tunnel. He picked up speed and headed for the seesaw. He ascended the ponderous apparatus, which tipped easily under his weight. He cleared two more jumps, jumped through the tire, and exited. The crowd jumped to their feet, cheering. He had completed the course. None of the last ten obstacles were in the correct order, but he'd done it in style.

As Liam exited the ring, he overheard a voice from the sidelines. "The bugger needs tae learn th' rules. 'At's a clever dug. With proper handlin' 'e could be somethin'."

27 Loonies and Toonies

The paper currency looks like Monopoly money: Queens instead of Presidents, loons instead of eagles, pastel pinks, blues, and greens. Unlike the U.S. dollar coin, the Canadian counterpart is easily distinguished from a quarter. It's affectionately called a "Loonie" because a swimming loon is stamped into the reverse side. Canada also has a two-dollar coin affectionately called "Two Loonies" or a "Twoonie." It looks like a quarter-sized washer with a brass center. The obverse side has a likeness of Elizabeth II, and the reverse shows a polar bear on an ice floe. Natives have shortened the spelling to "Toonie." French Canadians call the coin a "Polar."

After a weekend dog trial in Calgary, Liam and Cassy spent the next three days camping in the Canadian Rockies. Liam paid part of his camping fee with a two-dollar bill that he had squirreled away from a trip to Canada in the seventies.

The Ranger accepted it, wide-eyed. "Haven't seen one of these in years! I don't think the government prints two-dollar bills anymore, but it's still legal tender."

"Would that make it a collectors' item? What's it worth?" asked Liam.

"Oh, about a dollar fifty," the ranger deadpanned.

"Is there a two-dollar coin?"

"That would be a Toonie. Some wags call it a Moonie, because it has the Queen on one side with a bear behind. The early models had the center separate unexpectedly. Those are collector's items."

"The center may pop out? If someone hammered the center out, would that make it a collector's item?"

"Well, that would be against the law, but be careful not to freeze a Toonie or the center may eject."

Cassy giggled. "Thanks. We'll keep our money away from the freezer."

After a week in Canada, the campers needed showers and a chance to do laundry, but couldn't pass up a stop at Lake Louise in Banff National Park. The color of the alpine lake water varied from blue in the spring to turquoise green as the summer progressed. The unusual hue is produced by rock flour draining into the lake from the Victoria glacier on the surrounding mountains.

The melt waters from the nearby mountains drain off the continental divide to three oceans: the Atlantic, the Pacific, and the Arctic. A magnificent chateau housed guests from around the world in opulent splendor. Most of the tourists appeared to be dressed for elegant dining rather than mountain hiking.

Storm and Myst slept in the locked van while Cassy and Liam walked to the chateau. He stepped nimbly out of the way of a middle-aged Japanese woman in high heels and a fashionable print dress, who was trying to photograph a bird.

"Bird's name, please?" she asked politely in halting English.

Liam puffed up with pride because she'd picked the ideal person to answer her question. Fortunately, he'd seen that bird many times. "Clark's Nutcracker."

"Nutcracker?"

"Clark's Nutcracker."

"Oh, thank you, thank you." She moved closer to the bird to get a better picture. Liam remained pleased with himself until Cassy pointed out a few minutes later that it was a Canadian Jay.

"Are you sure?"

"Well, there's an information board behind you with the bird's picture and name on it."

Liam tried to redeem himself. "Maybe it's the Canadian name of the bird."

"Let's take a look at the chateau," Cassy suggested.

Flowers surrounded the entrance in a sea of colors. Valets scurried about, parking cars. Men in suits and ties and finely groomed women moved leisurely into and out of the archway entrance. Liam and Cassy weren't dressed for high society, but pretended to be guests and walked boldly inside. They passed a row of shops with prices for beautiful alpine sweaters, hats, jewelry, and other items that only people with money burning a hole in their pockets would be able to buy. Business was brisk.

Cassy said, "I'll be back in a minute. I'm going to use the restroom."

Liam hadn't shaved in a few days and felt uncomfortable in the pretentious surroundings, but walked over to a tourist booth and studied the guided excursions for the day. A cheerful young woman behind the desk asked, "Can I help you?"

Pretending to be a tourist with means, he replied, "What do you suggest?"

"Well, we have a six-hour bus trip to the Columbia glaciers, where you can transfer to a snow truck that drives out onto the glacier. Lunch is included."

"That sounds like fun."

"It's only $120."

"Is that for one or two people?"

"For one, of course. Canadian, not U.S."

Liam sensed the clerk realized he might be a deadbeat, so he didn't ask if he could bring a couple of dogs on the tour. "I'll check with my friend, thank you."

When Cassy returned, they left the chateau, again passing the Japanese woman, who smiled, half bowed, and proudly declared, "Clark's Nutcracker."

Liam forced a smile and gave a halfhearted affirmative nod. As they approached the parking lot, he excused himself and used a less elegant restroom provided for the hikers.

Leaving the National Park, they drove south toward Idaho along a rugged-looking wild river. They were surprised to learn the Columbia flowed north into Canada. How it ever found its way into Washington State and the Pacific Ocean puzzled them.

They stopped for lunch and let the dogs splash around in the shallow water near shore. Storm seemed impervious to the cold water. They loaded the wet dogs in the van and continued south to Cranbrook. About an hour from the border, Liam took stock of his Canadian money stash and counted ninety dollars and some change.

"Why don't we spend the rest of this Canadian money? Otherwise, it'll just gather dust at home. I'll get gas. Here's fifty dollars. Can you buy groceries?"

"What do we need?"

"About fifty dollars worth."

"I meant…" She paused. "Okay, there's a supermarket across from the gas station."

Liam passed a hand full of change and some bills to her. "Try to spend it all. No sense taking Canadian money into Idaho."

"Got it."

After carefully watching the gas pump until it said $41.16, Liam paid the attendant all the Canadian money he had left. He returned in time to hear Storm retching river water and green sand on the floor of the van. Liam had finished cleaning up the mess by the time Cassy returned with the groceries. She smiled smugly and announced, "I had to return a loaf of bread, but I spent all the money except for eighty-five cents."

"Good job."

At the border, they pulled over and parked at the duty free shop. "Let me have your 85 cents. I'm going to spend all our Canadian money before we cross the border."

"Liam, are you getting a little anal about this?"

"Probably…it'll just take a minute."

Liam hurried into the shop and quickly scanned the possibilities, choosing a postcard in the shape of a moose for 95 cents. "Can I pay for this with Canadian and U.S. money?" he asked.

The clerk gave him a curious look, but responded, "We can do that."

"Is there any tax?"

"No, this is a duty free shop."

"Okay, here's 85 cents Canadian, and ten cents American. That's 95 cents."

"First we'll have to convert the American cents to Canadian." The clerk adjusted his glasses. "Let me put that into the computer."

"I don't care. You can have the entire ten cents."

"No, let's do this right. Here we go. That'll be 85 cents Canadian, seven cents U.S. Here's your three cents change. Do you want a bag for this?"

Liam glanced at the three people waiting in line behind him. "No, that's okay."

"You better have a bag. Here's your receipt. I'll have someone drive this to the border for you."

"That's okay. I'll take it myself," Liam said, trying to resist the temptation to lay his head on the counter.

"No, it has to be declared. It won't be long. There'll be a car leaving very soon."

When he returned to the van, Cassy said, "Well, show me what you got."

"There's a car taking it to the border. Don't ask."

They drove the last 50 yards to the border. While waiting in line, Liam explained what had happened. The car with the postcard arrived, and they moved forward to the check station. After declaring they had no drugs or guns, Liam declared the postcard, and the guard let them into the United States.

Liam smiled smugly. He had spent all their Canadian money. He fumbled in his right-hand jacket pocket and pulled out four coins: the three Lincoln pennies received in change from the duty free shop, and a coin that looked like a quarter-sized washer with a brass center – a Toonie. He slumped and shut his eyes for a second.

The laughter coming from the passenger seat jolted him back to reality. Liam snorted air, half from his mouth and half from his nose, and joined in with convulsive laughter, a noise so alarming that the dogs began to bark.

"Well?" Cassy asked.

"Well, what?"

"Let me see the postcard."

28 Diving Dogs

Thursday morning Liam opened the front door. Storm raced to the curb, retrieved the newspaper, and bounced back to the house. He had trouble on Sundays. The ads and supplements were often spread out across the lawn. Pouring rain didn't bother him. The love of water was firmly embedded in his genes. If the morning paper were late, he'd simply cruise up and down the block until he found one on a neighbor's driveway. Liam would give him a biscuit and return the paper to the proper driveway.

Before getting dressed, Liam absentmindedly locked himself in the "reading room" with the sports section. His ex-wife used to knock on the door after twenty minutes in a vain attempt to roust him out. "Aren't you done yet? Did you fall in?"

Nineteen minutes into the sports section, an item caught his eye. The Purina Incredible Dog Challenge was coming to San Francisco. This made-for-TV special featured dogs and their handlers involved in goofy activities like wiener dog races, Frisbee competitions, and agility. Storm was pretty good at agility, but never quite good enough to get invited.

The last paragraph in the story got Liam's attention. The public was invited on Friday to try out for three spots in the finals of the Diving Dog competition. The other seven spots had already been selected. Storm liked to dive into the river in Idaho on the hot days; perhaps he could qualify.

Later that morning, he drove to Sebastopol with his plans.

"Liam, are you nuts?" Cassy said.

"We can do this. Tryouts are tomorrow, and the finals are on Saturday. Do you remember this summer at camp how Storm dove off the river bank to retrieve tennis balls?"

"You're serious, aren't you?"

"The dogs run down a platform and dive into a tank of water."

She looked unconvinced. "Why don't you admit it? You just want to be on TV."

"No. Well, maybe. It'll be on a cable network. Wouldn't you like to see us on TV? The entrants get a free T-shirt."

"Well, there you go. You can always use another T-shirt."

Ben listened quietly, looking somewhat amused. Lately, he had started taking Liam's side, as long as the issue was unimportant. "Well, I think you should go for it, as long as you're currently unemployed. It'll give you something to do. Keep you out of trouble."

Friday morning, Liam parked at Sharon Meadows in Golden Gate Park. Several huge tents had been erected in the area for vendors. A large crowd gathered to watch a police dog demonstration taking place in the main ring. After asking several official-looking sorts who could offer no help, he stopped by the Purina Dog Chow tent and registered in the Diving Dog Competition, scheduled to begin at 11 a.m.

Back at the van, he searched for a leash in a pile of sleeping bags, assorted dog toys, fishing equipment he'd used in

Idaho that summer, and some other things he didn't recognize anymore. Storm bolted out the open door, but Liam managed to catch his collar just in time to keep him from joining a nearby Frisbee game.

They walked past the Jack Russell Terrier hurdle races to a thirty-foot long tank of water. A young man with shoulder-length hair was smoking a cigarette while looking over the facility. His loose shirt hung over baggy pants with holes in the knees. He had a large, dark brown, shorthaired dog.

"Is that a Chesapeake Bay retriever?" Liam asked.

The young man took two quick puffs on his cigarette. "Yeh, dude. I think so. His name is Elvis. Are you entered in this gig?"

"I'm Liam. How about yourself?"

"Right as rain. I'm Josh. Can you win money at this thing?"

"No, but the winner gets all expenses paid to the finals in St. Louis."

"Sweet. I've never been to Iowa."

Storm put his front feet on the young man's chest and sniffed his jacket. Liam ordered his dog down. "I'm sorry. He probably smells food in your pocket."

"No, he probably smells my stash. He could be a drug sniffer at rock concerts."

Liam glanced at Josh's hand-rolled cigarette, which evidently was not tobacco. Given his recent troubles with the law, he figured it might be prudent to get the hell out of there. He looked nervously around, but no one seemed to be paying attention to them. "Good luck to you and Elvis. We're going to look around some more."

Shortly before eleven, Liam joined the entrants at the water tank for instructions. A large crowd of a several hundred people was gathered around the tank. Each dog got three jumps. The top three would join seven others pre-selected for the finals on the next day.

When his turn came, Liam walked Storm up a short flight of stairs to a twenty-foot long deck, where the dogs got a running start before leaping into the tank. Their leaping distance measured from the tip of their nose when they splashed in the water back to their launching spot. Each time a dog splashed, wild cheering erupted.

Liam put his dog in a sit-stay and walked to the edge of the platform. He tossed a tennis ball high over the water and yelled, "Come." Storm charged down the runway, but stopped momentarily, surprised to see water in front of him. His momentum caused him to lose his balance, and he fell in the water. Once in the water, he felt right at home and swam strongly toward the ball.

The upbeat announcer made the call. "Let's hear it for the flat-coated retriever and his handler Liam Gallagher. The jump was 18 inches."

Storm began swimming laps around the tank with the ball in his mouth, determined to enjoy his swim. No amount of coaxing could get him out of the water. Several times he swam by just out of Liam's reach.

The announcer milked the comedy. "It appears the dog is having more fun than his handler would like. Mr. Gallagher may have to go into the tank to get his dog."

Liam started descending the stairs into the tank. The water was up to his knees before he managed to catch Storm's collar as he swam by. The crowd gave them a Bronx cheer. Once out of the water, Storm proceeded to shake in full body, high-speed oscillations, whipping water in all directions.

This effective drying mechanism has been estimated to disperse half the water in less than a second, and is more effective than a washing machine's spin cycle.

After that first round, Storm was positioned in twelfth place in the fifteen-dog field. He led three dogs that had refused to jump in the water at all. Clearly, Liam needed a new strategy. Back at the van, he found a fishing pole and rigged a heavy line attached to the tennis ball. He practiced a few times fly-casting the ball.

Liam climbed the deck stairs for round two. He commanded his dog to stay and moved forward a step with the fishing rod. He glimpsed a black blur charging toward him and grabbed the breakaway collar, which broke under the stress of trying to hold back a seventy-pound dog. In desperation, he grabbed his tail. The crowd murmured disapprovingly, but Storm seemed hardly phased by his correction.

Liam snapped the collar back in place and tried again. He walked slowly forward. "Staaay, Staaay." Storm flinched to start, and Liam put out his right hand to stop him. "Staaay."

Liam moved forward four steps before his dog broke. Liam raced to the water's edge and flicked the fishing pole, sending the tennis ball airborne five feet over the water. Storm leaped high in the air trying to snap his mouth around the ball. He just missed but landed well out into the water. He retrieved the ball and again began swimming victory laps. Liam carefully reeled in the line, grabbed the collar and triumphantly pulled Storm out of the water.

The announcer proclaimed, "Fourteen feet, six inches! That moves Storm into eighth place. Our next dog is Elvis, currently in fifth place."

The energized crowd shouted, "El-vis! El-vis!"

Josh told Elvis to stay and walked casually to the edge of the tank. His dog sat rock solid, like a statue. Josh tossed a red rubber bumper toy well out into the water. "Elvis, get it."

Elvis exploded like a spring suddenly released and charged down the runway. He launched into the air, a picture of grace, with his front legs tucked backward and his hind legs tucked forward. When he hit the water, the splash cascaded into the third row of spectators.

"El-vis! El-vis!" screamed the crowd.

"Twenty feet, four inches! That moves Elvis into second place!" came the announcement.

After Josh and Elvis cleared the competition area, Liam congratulated him. "Way to go. That was awesome. How did you train Elvis to jump like that?"

Josh was higher than...well, than he had been that morning. "Thanks, Dude. We train at my house in Atherton. Elvis always gets a big kick catching Frisbees when I throw them over the pool. That fishing pole thing is so cool. It got your drug-sniffing dog to jump up instead of flattening."

Liam was surprised the young man with holes in his jeans called upscale Atherton his home. "Would you like to borrow it for the last round? I could help out. I'll bet Elvis could go over 21 feet."

"Oh, excellent. Sweet. Can I offer you a smoke?"

"'No, thanks. Tell you what. I'll work the pole for Elvis and would you do the same when it's our turn?"

"No problem, dude."

Josh and Liam practiced their fishing pole technique on the grass. They concluded the secret to success seemed to be casting the suspended tennis ball high over the water, and having the dogs jump high rather than simply lurching forward.

As planned during round three, Josh moved to the end of the runway with the fishing pole. It took all of Liam's strength to hold on to Storm who kept lunging forward. When released, he tore down the runway and launched high into the air, snapping at the tennis ball, which Josh flicked out over the water. The retriever hit the water swimming, with a powerful stroke. The crowd noise cheered him on. He exited the tank and shook water over a ten-foot area.

"Nineteen feet, ten inches. That moves Storm into fifth place."

Liam was thrilled. They hadn't qualified for the finals on Saturday, but he liked his dog's enthusiasm.

The announcer worked the energized crowd. "Our last dog is currently in second place. Let's hear it for Elvis!"

"El-vis! El-vis! El-vis!"

As they agreed, Liam held the fishing pole while Josh positioned his dog for his last jump. Elvis sat rock solid, his dark eyes focused with laser intensity. Josh gave the signal, and the Chesapeake Bay retriever exploded down the runway. All present were mesmerized at his power as he bore down toward Liam who almost forgot what he needed to do. Jolted back to attention, he flicked the fishing pole and the ball went flying far out over the water. Elvis took off and flew through the air. He appeared to be moving in slow motion, defying the law of gravity, like a broad jumping Jesse Owens. He made the impossible look easy. It appeared he would never come down. The crowd grew quiet watching this flying machine in the air. They held their breath. Finally, Elvis hit the water barely a few feet from the back edge of the tank. The splash cascaded deep into the crowd, like a killer whale show at Marine World, where the best seats received the most water when the leviathans smacked the surface after incredible leaps. The roar was deafening. A thousand starstruck groupies screamed, "EL-VIS! EL-VIS!"

"Twenty-eight feet, three inches. That's less than one foot from the world record. Elvis moves into first place!"

"Wah-hoo! I'm going to Iowa!" screamed Josh. He did a front flip into the water tank and swam a victory lap with his dog. Liam helped Josh out of the water and reminded him that he still had to win on Saturday, and that St. Louis was actually in Missouri.

Liam arrived on Saturday with his fishing pole ready to assist. Unfortunately, Elvis missed the finals and a chance to travel to Missouri or even Iowa. A rumor had it that Josh had celebrated long into the night and was in no condition to compete. The fourth place finisher from the day before moved into the finals. Storm, in fifth place, missed the adjusted qualifying spot by one place. The winning dog that day jumped a respectable 26 feet.

29 Cage

California has a Mediterranean climate. Winter rains give way to spring wildflowers: blue-eyed grass, lupine, and Indian paintbrush. When the rain ends, the grass dies. The wildflowers go to seed. It's inevitable. It's cyclic.

The Sierra foothills in August were covered with dry brown grass. Californians like to call the color golden. Cassy had flown to Alaska to see her mother, who had been hospitalized. Late Friday afternoon, Liam arrived alone at the Tuolumne County Fairgrounds. While he unloaded his van, he listened to Stuart Conner hold court with two young female admirers.

Stuart, barely thirty, had already won a national championship with his border collie, Frenzy. A former soccer player, his athletic skill was a good match for his speedy canine partner.

Jennifer and Britney basked in the attention they were receiving from the tall, lean champion. They hung on his every word. Both had attended agility camp in May, and they proudly wore baggy souvenir T-shirts reminiscent of that experience. Stuart called them the "C" girls, short for camp girls, because that's mostly what they talked about. If you looked carefully, you could tell them apart. Jennifer had purple streaks in her side ponytail; Britney had green.

"Britney and me are so excited about this weekend," Jennifer gushed. "This weekend is going to be so cool. Like I hope I don't look like a total dweeb."

"Just relax and focus on what you've learned," Stuart assured her. "You and Buster can be awesome."

"Ohmygod. Like I'm so nervous. Do you really think so?"

"Just remember to keep your eyes on your dog when you're in the ring."

"Right. I just freak when Buster starts shooting all over the place. I'm like Hellooo Buster. There's two of us out here. We're supposed to be a team."

The object of her adulation replied, "It takes time to be a good handler."

"You are so right. Who's the best handler you ever saw?"

Stuart hesitated and broke into a mischievous smile. "Well, modesty prevents me from—"

"Ohmygod. Gimme a break. I mean besides you."

"The best handler I ever saw? There's a guy in the San Fernando Valley who's good." Stuart paused. "And another guy who used to compete with a pug."

"Shut up! A pug? You're messing with me. I mean a pug can hardly breathe, and like they've got this little smashed face. I mean they're cute but…"

When Jennifer paused to breathe, Britney broke in. "Yeah, he's messing with you. Come on. Let's get our tent ready."

"Bye, Stuart." Jennifer giggled as she and Britney left.

Saturday morning at 7:30, the competitors gathered in the cool morning mist. Liam recognized Simon and Emily Frazier from the Idaho camp that summer. Simon had recently turned seventy and didn't move as well as he once did, but he still competed with a ballistic Aussie that would be difficult for someone half his age to handle. Emily wrote corny agility songs meant to be sung to the melodies of old favorites, like "Clementine."

Emily turned to Liam. "Good morning. Too bad about Cage, isn't it?"

Surprised, Liam asked, "What's that?"

"His pug, Sophie, died Thursday night. He was supposed to be here this weekend, but I haven't seen him."

Liam shook his head. "What was she? About fourteen?"

"Fifteen, I think."

Liam knew a little about Cage. He had grown up on a farm in Oklahoma and later worked for the California Highway Department near Bakersfield. He was a pioneer in the sport of dog agility, and his first dog was a pug named Sophie. The fearless little dog became his first agility champion. Cage's next dog was a sheepherding border collie named Turlock. He also handled Shooter, a terrier, for his girlfriend, Joan. She was always at the trials supporting him, although the disease that tormented him for many years must have been a terrible strain on her.

"I think Cage had a special place in his heart for Sophie," Emily went on.

Liam nodded. "He told me at a trial that she was nearly blind the last few years, but still managed to keep Turlock in his place. He asked me once how to break Sophie from wolfing down horse poop. That was one skill Cage could never teach her. I told him to sprinkle pepper on the horse manure. If the dog ate it, the problem would be cured forever. A few weeks later he told me, 'I ain't never gonna take your advice again. I used pepper like you told me, and now all my dogs are wild for Cajun horse poop!'"

Emily passed around song sheets before the entrants prepared for the first event, a distance test called Gamblers. The group sang while Simon played "Clementine" on his accordion.

> Oh, my good dog, such a good dog
> Runs the courses so divine
> If she only had a handler
> That was equally as fine

Liam glanced around self-consciously and pretended to sing. Most of the women eagerly joined in. He noted that women, generally, were more at ease acting a little silly. Simon cranked up his accordion for one last chorus.

> Oh, my good dog did the Gamble
> Did the Gamble just in time
> But we lost a leg that morning
> When my foot went o'er the line

Everyone cheered as Simon finished with a flourish. A woman yelled in her best boxing announcer voice, "Let's get ready to Gamble."

Simon had told Liam a story about Cage. "At the North American Championships in Olympia, Washington, the Gamble had been set up in three tiers. While the handler stayed behind the line, the dog could be directed to near obstacles for single points, a farther second tier for double points, or the third tier about thirty yards away for triple points. In the extraordinary competition that day, the large dogs played 'can you top this?' The scores hit sixty, eighty, then one hundred points. Turlock ran last.

"When the whistle blew, Cage sent the border collie out as if he were gathering sheep. He gathered triple points instead. He'd amassed one hundred twenty points to win the event. That night they celebrated by going out to dinner. Before entering the restaurant, a friend whispered to Simon not to order anything alcoholic. For the first time he became aware of the demons haunting Cage."

One of the first teams in the ring Saturday morning was Jennifer and her sheltie, Buster. The little dog tore around the ring at mach speed. Jennifer tried desperately to keep up. She failed to see hurdle number six and crashed into it at full speed. She lay on the ground while Buster stood over her barking. Stuart entered the ring and helped her up.

"Are you okay?"

"Sure. Just a couple broken legs!" she responded tearfully. "I am so embarrassed. I'm quitting and going home!"

"No, you're not. Don't be a quitter. You did some nice things out there, and you've got Buster really motivated. You remember the guy with the pug I told you about?"

"Oh, please. Don't start."

"Besides the pug, he also had a border collie. One time, he fell in the ring just like you did. He lay there laughing and directed his dog around the rest of the course yelling the names of the obstacles and giving left and right directions. He not only had a clean run but won the event."

Jennifer frowned. "Oh, that makes me feel a lot better."

Later that afternoon, Jennifer and Buster had a fast clean run on the novice Jumpers course. Everyone watching cheered except Emily, who walked over to Liam, teary-eyed. "I thought you should know…we've lost Cage."

"What do you mean?"

"He must have felt pretty low the night Sophie passed on. Alone, I'm afraid the demons came back to visit. A neighbor found him Friday morning. He'd fallen off his deck to a cement patio and hit his head. He was in a coma…brain dead. This morning he passed away."

Liam stood there, stunned. He put his arms around Emily, who sobbed. His eyes welled with tears and a blink sent them running down his cheeks.

That evening a small group assembled near the well-watered agility ring, with its lush green grass. Liam gazed at the waning light on the surrounding hills, golden in the setting sun. We don't think much about life's small joys until they're gone, he thought.

One by one, those present remembered Cage. There were stories about Cajun poop, and how he used to carry his girl friend's terrier upside down to the starting line. Simon played "Amazing Grace" on his accordion. There must have been a lot of pollen in the air, because eyes were getting moist.

That night, Liam sat outside at his campsite and stared at the sky. The full moon rising in the east cast a silvery glow on the fairgrounds. The starlight he viewed had originated billions of years before in distant galaxies. His lifetime was a mere nanosecond compared to the age of the universe. Storm put his head in his lap, and Liam stroked the soft, smooth, furry head, content in their nanosecond.

30 The Summer of Love

The Beechcraft turboprop cruised low above the Kenai Peninsula on the final approach to Homer, 110 miles south of Anchorage. Cassy gazed out at the generously spaced homesteads separating the Sterling Highway from the sheer cliffs of the coastline. The highway ended in Homer, the last outpost of the Alaskan frontier. She could see people in one yard waving at the plane. Maybe they knew her mother?

Homer became the last stop in Sandy O'Neil's odyssey after she dropped out of mainstream America. She began her exodus from stifling suburbia in the sixties, when she quit high school and moved to the North Beach district of San Francisco. Later she moved to Haight-Ashbury. She wore a flower in her hair and danced barefoot to flute music in Golden Gate Park. The 1967 Summer of Love started out well, but morphed into something else. One hundred thousand newcomers descended upon the city: war protesters, college students, drug experimenters, and runaways. Sandy and her friends fled to New Mexico to create a new Shangri-La. Cassy was born on the day Neil Armstrong first walked on the moon. Sandy gave up on the failed New Mexico Utopia in 1983 and moved with her daughter to Cotati, California. After the Exxon Valdez oil spill in 1989, Sandy joined volunteers rescuing oil-soaked otters in Prince Edward Sound. She cleaned birds and cleaned up her drug habit at the same time.

After being home-schooled in New Mexico, Cassy felt like an outsider entering high school as a junior. She didn't fit in with the other girls, with their crimped hair, hot pink makeup, skin-tight acid-washed jeans with ripped-out knees, and Members Only jackets. Suppressed anger compelled her to act out in ways she didn't understand. Mrs. Kowalski, her English teacher, was the only person who seemed really interested in her. She remembered reading George Orwell's *Animal Farm*. "Some animals are more equal than others." She crossed out the sentence with a black marking pen. A dozen years later, the missing pieces of her life were finally falling into place, except one. Who was her father?

The Smokey Bear Air shuttle made an uneventful landing and taxied to the terminal. She saw her mom at the base of the passenger ramp, smiling. Sandy, always thin, now appeared gaunt, older than her fifty plus years, her skin weathered from years in the sun.

Cassy exited and moved quickly to the tarmac. They hugged for several seconds. Sandy wiped tears from her eyes.

"Honey, I'm so happy to see you. How was your flight?"

"Wonderful. The scenery was beautiful, the snow on the mountains, the dark water. So…how have you been?"

"There are good days and bad days."

"Do you remember the freeway battles you had in San Francisco?"

Sandy laughed. "Of course. We pretty much shut those projects down."

"Well, I'm staying with a Mr. Kowalski. He was the engineer who tried to get them built."

"I'll be damned. I remember him. How'd that happen?"

"It's a long story. Anyway, he's offered to fly you to San Francisco and pay for treatment at Stanford."

"Now why would he do that?"

"I've been taking care of him, and he wants to give back in some way."

Sandy shook her head. "Funny how things work out. Life is too short to carry around some long ago rancor. That's awfully nice of him, but I have a friend who flies me to Anchorage every few weeks. I'll get by."

"Think about it some more."

"Okay. Let's go home."

Cassy plopped her bag into the bed of her mom's truck. They took the obligatory tourist route home on the four-and-a-half mile Homer Spit Road, passing fish joints, halibut charters, rowdy bars, and souvenir shops. After a U-turn they headed west through the congested downtown, which was sprinkled with artists' galleries, restaurants, and inspiring views of the Bay and the mountains. They continued on the Sterling highway and arrived twenty minutes later at Sandy's pleasant little three-bedroom home. Cassy admired the view of the Bay. She noticed an ample supply of firewood piled neatly within easy walking distance of the back door.

"Mom, you're amazing. How can you keep this place up, firewood and all?"

"I'm pushing sixty, but I'm not senile. You have to be able to take care of yourself up here. The neighbors are always ready to help, if needed. Jack takes care of the heavy stuff."

"Wait a minute. Who's Jack?"

"Jack's my housemate. He's up in Prudhoe Bay right now. He flies down every few weeks."

"Is he in the oil business?"

"Yeah, we get a lot of traffic through our airport. Sometimes I think I'll have to move again, but I'm getting too old for that. Tell me about this Mr. Kowalski you're staying with."

"Well, to start with he's eighty-eight."

"So I assume he's not your love interest."

"There's this guy I've been seeing…a teacher. I've got a secret I have to tell you."

Sandy did a double take. "You're pregnant?"

Cassy rolled her eyes. "God, no. Did you ever know your biological mother?"

"No, never particularly thought it important."

"Weren't you curious?"

Sandy paused. "Maybe. The O'Neil's did the best they could for me. I'll always be thankful to them, although I had to get out. In high school I used to sneak out on weekends and go to North Beach."

"North Beach. San Francisco. Hippies, am I right?"

"Hippies came later. I wanted to be a Beat."

"A Beatnik?"

"No, Beats. Herb Caen of the Chronicle invented the word Beatnik later, a reference to the Russian space satellite, Sputnik. I hung around the coffee shops and listened to Ginsberg's poetry. I met Jack Kerouac and Neal Cassidy. Even saw Bob Dylan once. After high school, I wanted to be on my own. My friends went to college. I moved to North Beach."

"Well, that must have been exciting, trying to change the world."

"The Beats weren't trying to change the world. They tried to create a counterculture as a reaction to mainstream fifties. The Beatles were influenced by the Beats." She paused, deep in thought. "You mentioned my biological mother."

"So you are curious."

Sandy feigned a hurt look. "Don't be a tease."

"This older gentleman I'm staying with married her after the war."

"Wow! That's weird. How do you know that?"

"Your mom's name was Rebecca. She told him the whole story…about you, the O'Neil's, everything. She got pregnant and dropped out of high school. Your father enlisted in the army and died in Sicily during the war. She got her GED, graduated from Berkeley, and became a teacher. My high school English teacher."

Sandy took a deep breath. "I remember her. You liked her a lot, didn't you?"

"Yeah. I looked her up a year ago in Sebastopol, but she had died. Her husband knew all about you and me, and let me stay with him while he recovered from a heart attack."

"So that explains why he wanted to help with my medical bills."

"I guess. So what do you say? Why don't you come live with us? Think it over."

"You're thirty years old. It's about time I shared a secret with you. I've got all the money I need. This house is paid for, and I've got plenty to get me through for years."

"Okay, now I'm curious."

"There was this guy, Billie Cunningham from Newport, Rhode Island. He came to San Francisco during the Summer of Love, and I moved in with him. The newcomers ruined it for us. They turned the city into a zoo…drugs, sex, testing the system. They used peace and love as a cover. Tourists came in buses to take pictures. I had to get out, and Billie wanted to go with me."

Cassy's heart raced. She felt smothered, as if the room's air had been purged of oxygen. She could hear her own raging heartbeat and felt a paralyzing lightheadedness. She managed to whisper, "Are you telling me…"

"He dropped out of Brown University, and we left for New Mexico that year. He's your father. Shortly after you were born, his family pressured him to come home and finish college. He insisted on providing the support I needed to raise you."

Cassy felt a sudden chill. "Why didn't you ever tell me?"

Sandy swallowed hard. "Over the years, the checks kept coming. I heard he ran for Congress. I wanted to join him, but his family forbid it. I got a final big check in the mail from his mother." Sandy's voice cracked, and her eyes filled with tears. "I wanted to tear it up, but I'm ashamed to say I didn't. I knew it wouldn't work out." She took a deep breath. "He served four terms. I've always felt guilty. I took the money and did whatever I could to make this a better world. Every time I washed oil off a duck, I felt better." She touched Cassy's hand. "If you find the right person, promise me you'll fight for him."

Cassy's eyes welled with tears. "I promise."

31 Phoenix

The North American Dog Agility Championships: Day 1

The sides of the covered horse pavilion were open. An occasional breeze carried torrid desert air across the dirt floor of the competition area. Cassy's auburn hair was caked with sweat around her ears and forehead. Younger than most of the other competitors, her slight build and running background gave her an edge in the desert heat.

She finished a bottle of water to ease the dryness in her mouth, took a deep breath, and entered the warm-up area. She wished Liam was there, but he had a court appearance. She had weathered storms in the branches of a redwood tree. She could handle this competition.

The sounds of the announcer droned on over the public address. Past events and images raced through Cassy's mind. Myst was generally considered to be a "soft" dog. Their dismal collapse on the final day of the California Cup competition in San Jose replayed in the back of her mind.

Nearby, Preston Wadsworth attended to Ringo. Raising his voice loud enough for Cassy to hear, he nodded toward Myst and told his female companion, "That border collie is a loser. Always has been, always will be."

"You bastard," Cassy muttered to herself.

Cassy and Myst entered the ring for the first of eight rounds. Each team ad-libbed the opening sequence of the Gamblers course for points: one point for jumps, three for tunnels and the tire, five for the contact obstacles and the weave poles. She would hear a whistle after forty seconds. At that time, she needed to stay behind a distance line and send Myst away for fifteen seconds. Nearby obstacles were worth double points, distant obstacles triple points.

She remembered the advice she received at the Idaho camp. The distance line was not your friend. The magic word and key to distance handling was space. Sometimes, handler and dog must share space, but moving abruptly into the dog's space will drive it away. Most handlers were tempted to hug the line closely and keep their dogs as near as possible, but that restricted their movement, making it impossible to control the dog at great distances.

The clerk quietly commanded, "Go when ready."

Cassy and Myst crossed the start line, took two nearby jumps to gather speed, and entered the part of the course with high-value obstacles. Cassy planned a flowing, curving sequence to maintain maximum speed: weave poles, A-frame, teeter, dog walk, and tunnels.

She worked her dog back toward the distance line and positioned herself several feet behind that line as the first whistle blew. She charged forward with her left arm extended. "Out!" Myst moved away through a series of tunnels and jumps. Cassy's subtle movements of arms, feet, and shoulders directed the dog, taking advantage of its sheepherding instincts.

"Out!" Myst moved farther away, working the distant objects worth triple points.

A second whistle blew, and they crossed the finish line. Later she checked the scores: 102 points. First place. Early that afternoon, they ran round two, another Gamblers course, and won with 97 points. Myst remained in first place, eight points ahead of Preston Wadsworth and Ringo.

The temperature pressed beyond the century mark, suspending the competition until eight that night. The last event on Friday was a Jumpers course: twenty-four jumps and two tunnels that tested the ability of handlers to maintain tight control of their dog.

By 10 p.m., the temperature had mercifully dropped below one hundred degrees. As each dog/handler pair finished, they fled the building, because they knew they needed to return the following morning at daybreak. By midnight, the pavilion was nearly deserted except for the few dozen entries remaining. To no one's surprise, Preston Wadsworth and Ringo, the masters of tight control, had a fast time with no faults.

Because Cassy and Myst were leading after the two Gamblers runs, they were the last of the dogs to compete. Shortly before 1 a.m. on Saturday morning, they entered the ring. Thirty seconds, and one ten-fault off course later, they had dropped to second place.

32 Crash & Burn

The North American Dog Agility Championships: Day 2

The key to Myst's rapid improvement had been clicker training. Dogs were conditioned to clicks like Pavlov's dog was to a bell. Once conditioned to the clicker, the rest of the training fell quickly into place. Training became play. Training clicks replaced the electric shocks administered by Preston Wadsworth.

The afternoon temperature pushed well over the 100-degree mark. For the second day in a row, the competition was suspended and scheduled to resume at eight to avoid the afternoon heat.

The competition area was under a huge horse pavilion; the sides open to the hot desert breeze. Although this was the second day of the North American Championships, not all of the entries were still competing. Because of the heat, some simply gave up and pulled their dogs from the competition.

Round four, a Jumpers class, had been held Saturday morning. Myst ran clean and remained in second overall behind the usually reliable Ringo, who dropped a bar, which sliced his first place margin to two points. Preston and Ringo recovered during round five later on Saturday and upped their lead to twelve points.

A gust of dry, hot air blew through the arena. The sun had set two hours earlier, and the oppressive Phoenix heat finally began to dissipate. Cassy nervously attached the slip lead around her dog's neck and led her to a water hose to spray her tummy and feet. That was the routine: the water spray to cool off, a few practice jumps, and a practice set of six weave poles.

The dog sniffed the ground at nothing in particular and jumped playfully at a Corgi that darted by, chasing a ball. Then Myst rolled over onto her back, squirming back and forth, scratching her back. She was headed to the ring and her favorite activity. A year ago, she had been stressed before competitions, but now she relished the chance to run and work. Because of her herding instincts, she was hard-wired to work with her mistress.

Cassy felt herself calming down. I can do this, she told herself. She was oblivious to all around her, including Preston and Ringo, warming up behind her. She kneeled and patted Myst lightly. The announcer's voice droned on in the background. Her shoulders relaxed. She closed her eyes and mentally ran the course, unaware she was murmuring out loud. "Jump. Out. Switch."

Three classes remained: one that evening and two more on Sunday. They included all the regular obstacles and would test every skill of Myst and her handler. The courses would be fast, wide open, and flow smoothly from obstacle to obstacle, but they would be filled with obstacle discriminations or traps. If dogs were too fast, there could be off courses or dropped bars. Fast, out-of control dogs would crash and burn.

The first four obstacles were jumps in a straight line that brought dogs up to full speed. Next, dogs would race back and forth through three tunnels. The middle of the course included three contact obstacles and the weave poles. The finish included jumping through a tire and over three more jumps in a straight line to the finish.

Myst's strength was her consistency over the first five rounds: no displaced bars, no missed contacts, and only one off course. She ran round six fast with no faults, easily her best run of the competition.

As the leader, Ringo ran last, the final dog to run Saturday night. He ran flawlessly through the opening sequence of jumps and tunnels. Preston had perfect control. Ringo nailed the yellow zones on the contact obstacles and headed for the closing sequence, but the Aussie was running so fast that he drifted farther from his handler. JUMP. JUMP. JUMP. Preston screamed at his runaway Aussie.

Ringo, perhaps sensing his unfamiliar distance from his handler, turned back in midair and crashed into the last jump, sending the bar and the uprights flying. The judge signaled an unsafe performance – twenty faults. The team from Sebastopol, California was back in first place.

The North American Dog Agility Championships:
Final Day

Two courses remained. Myst ran clean in round seven in the morning, but lost a few seconds to Ringo. Her lead had been trimmed to five points, which equated to five seconds or perhaps a dropped bar. A ten-fault off course or a missed contact would be devastating. One round remained.

As round eight neared completion, all eyes shifted to the last two dog teams. The crowd's initial murmuring gave way to a nervous silence. Cassy had been in a similar position during the California Cup in San Jose, when she and Myst had a disastrous run, with off courses and missed contacts. She had heard unfriendly whispers that she had choked.

She tried to concentrate on the task ahead, but thought of Liam. Ben and her mother had once been antagonists in the San Francisco freeways battles. They both found peace by forgiving. Suddenly, she knew what she must do. Even though Myst's first owner, Preston, had mistreated the border collie, the time had come to forgive. She walked over to Preston and offered her hand. "Good luck," she said. "Ringo has been magnificent."

She felt liberated. Even Myst must have sensed the release of tension and wagged her tail. Preston seemed stunned and murmured absently, "Thanks. Good luck to you."

Preston and Ringo ran first with no errors. The timing clock flashed the time to beat in large red numbers for all to see. The last team would need a flawless run.

Cassy mentally reviewed the course. She felt calm and confident. She told Myst to stay on the start line, and led out to obstacle two.

Myst watched as Cassy walked slowly down the course. Her front legs quivered in anticipation until she heard the command to start. Accelerating to full speed, she jumped the first three hurdles and focused on Cassy's shoulders as they turned to the right.

"Thru."

The dog blasted through the first two tunnels and focused on the jump ahead.

"Out."

She moved quickly away from the jump ahead and entered the third tunnel. She followed Cassy's body language from several yards away and turned sharply left to the A-Frame. She raced up and down the A-Frame and temporarily froze on the bottom, her two front feet in the dirt and two hind feet in the yellow zone. Off running again. Cassy hesitated and then turned sharply toward the weave poles. The plastic poles bounced off the sides of Myst's body, first on the left and then on the right. She accelerated out between the eleventh and twelfth poles.

"Here."

She turned sharply toward Cassy, up, across, and down the dog walk. Myst again froze with her hind feet in the yellow zone. She jumped through the tire. Cassy was falling farther behind.

"Go on. Go!"

Myst, sixty feet ahead, streaked for the finish. Centuries of instinctive herding behavior controlled her now. She skimmed the last three jumps at full speed.

The roar of human voices was startling. Cassy jumped up and down, squealing. She shook when she picked Myst up. People ran toward them, jumping and yelling, hugging Cassy. Tears ran down her face.

Cassy led Myst from the ring, kicked off her shoes, removed her socks, and ripped off her sweat-soaked T-shirt. Attired now in shorts and a black sports bra, she passed Preston close enough to hear his female companion say, "Well. That was shocking."

Cassy turned and responded calmly. "No, we just clicked today."

Preston held out his hand. "Congratulations. You deserved to win today."

33 The Almost Perfect Storm

In November 1997 the North American Team Champion-ships took place at Stanford University in Palo Alto. This was the first time an agility trial had been held on the picturesque campus. Built as a mixture of mission and Romanesque architecture, Stanford is distinctly Californian. Located about forty-five minutes south of San Francisco, the campus is adorned by scenic foothills and mountain ranges to the west.

Myst, after her stunning upset victory in Phoenix the previous month, was scheduled to join a select team of three talented dogs, but unfortunately she came up limping after a Frisbee session. The vet diagnosed it as a possible soft tissue injury in her back. With no other blue-ribbon dogs available on such late notice, Liam and Storm were asked to fill in by the other members of the team. Four dogs comprised a team, but only the scores for the top three dogs in each round counted. The low score was dropped. As the fourth dog in the group, Storm's scores in the competition didn't seem too important. He offered insurance in case one of the speedy collies made a mistake.

The other members of the team were three lightning fast border collies: Bolt, Laser, and Oreo. Stacey Winters handled the tri-color female, Bolt, who jumped 20-inch hurdles. Stacy had wanted Myst to be on the same team as Bolt, but had seen Storm that summer in the Idaho camp and liked his steady performances. Two of Stacey's friends handled the other dogs. Oreo, a black and white female, competed in the twenty-inch jump group. Laser, a black and white male, competed at twenty-four inches, as did Storm. Besides the team competition, the individual winners at each jump height would be awarded trophies.

Storm's biggest problem had been knocking bars off the hurdles. His hind feet were lazy. Perhaps he thought, if they hit a cross bar, so what? It didn't hurt. His adrenaline level was so high that he was impervious to pain. He needed to become aware of his hind legs. It cost a quarter to solve the problem.

Liam picked up the training tip in Idaho. The elastic bands that girls use to hold their ponytails in place were pulled up over Storm's hocks during warm-ups. They weren't allowed in competition, so before entering the ring Liam had to remove them. The lingering feelings reminded the dog that he did in fact have hind legs that he needed to lift over the jumps.

The Outdoor Life cable network taped the Championships. Technicians set up small cameras in the tunnels and in other strategic places. A huge crane overhead followed the action. Cameras zoomed in on key obstacles, like the weave poles. A border collie ripping through twelve weave poles always drew an appreciative gasp from the crowd.

On the first day of competition, Liam took Storm on a potty break, an essential routine. If a dog eliminated in the ring, it got a zero.

An attractive coed in a red Stanford sweatshirt approached them. "What a beautiful dog! What is he? A Labrador retriever?"

Storm wiggled his whole body in perfect synchronization with his tail and made a noise, something like a blend of a snort and a squeal. His feet moved back and forth as if he were tap dancing.

"A flat-coated retriever," Liam said.

"I just love labs. Look how long his hair is."

"Not a lab, a flat-coat."

"A black coat? Is that a golden retriever mix of some kind?"

"Not black...flat. It's a separate breed."

"Can I pet him?"

"Sure."

The young woman knelt and made a big fuss over Storm, who responded by licking her face, jumping up, and nearly pushing her over.

"I'm sorry, he gets carried away sometimes." That wasn't entirely true. Storm got carried away every time.

"Oh, he's so friendly. Well, good luck this weekend."

"Thanks. Good luck to the Cardinal football team in today's Big Game with Cal."

As the weekend progressed, Bolt and Laser were sensational and led the competition in their respective jump height groups. Oreo had a few good runs but also a few disasters. Storm was steady and had perfect runs on Saturday. He seemed energized by the occasional roar drifting from the football stadium across the campus. His times weren't fast enough to place him with the leaders, but his consistency helped his team into first place.

The competition continued on Sunday. When Storm's last run was imminent, Liam took him on one last potty break. He heard a voice behind him. "Good luck. We beat Cal 21-20 yesterday!"

"Way to go!" he replied to the Stanford coed and, momentarily distracted, almost forgot to remove the warm-up elastic bands from his dog's legs. The last run would probably determine the team championship. Bolt and Laser had run moments before and were certain to win individual honors. Liam glanced at the TV camera that turned toward him as he walked to the start line. He heard the announcer say, "Next up is Storm, a flat-coated retriever, handled by Liam Gallagher from Santa Rosa, California."

The flat-coat lived for these moments and quivered in anticipation. He broke from the starting line with an energy level that was extraordinary even for him. He powered through the opening sequence. Jump, jump, tunnel. Up and down the teeter-totter in record time. Despite his amazing speed, he nailed the yellow zones on the dog walk and the A-frame. Two more jumps completed and no bars down. The TV camera zoomed in. Only two obstacles remained, but Storm slowed as he entered the weave poles. Left, right, left, right, pause, left, pause. He arched his back. He stopped. No! No! He was pooping. The TV camera pulled back. The judge signaled elimination. A zero.

When the team winners were announced, Storm's team hadn't even made the top three. Liam was numb. He should have been more careful. Perhaps he'd been distracted during the pre-run warm-up, but he refused to use that excuse. His partners tried to console him, but the anguish would be slow to dissipate.

A month later Liam received a large package in the mail. He could hardly believe his eyes as he removed the first place team trophy. There had been an error in the scoring. The scorekeepers had forgotten to drop Storm's zero in the last round and replace it with the score from the fourth member of the team, Oreo. Liam showed the trophy to his dog, whose feet danced with glee.

34 Carter Quarters and Double Eagles

Liam had applied for a track-coaching job at a private school on the Peninsula and had an interview the next day. The stipend would barely cover the cost of gas, but at least it would give him some focus for a while.

Sure, that weasel Frank had framed him, but the wheels of justice turn slowly. The shadow of impropriety tended to stick, like a misstep into doggie droppings.

The day before his interview, he made one of his increasingly frequent treks to Sebastopol. He should have called ahead, but he'd canceled his telephone service to save a few dollars. Perhaps a "just happened to be in the neighborhood" excuse would work, although this ploy was most likely wearing thin. That little white lie wasn't necessary when he saw Cassy's Datsun in the driveway.

Ben answered the door. "You just missed her. Caught a ride with this professor who's been hanging around a lot lately. How'd the Stanford gig go?"

She'd mentioned that guy before. Could anything else go wrong? He tried to collect himself. "We were doing pretty well until the last event. How was your weekend?"

"Terrible. Watched the Big Game. We had those SOBs trapped inside the ten, fourth down with 20 seconds to play.

All Cal needed was a field goal, but Stanford took an intentional safety, punted out of danger, and won by a point. We'd have kicked their butts in OT."

"Yeah. Too bad." Liam barely heard Ben. All he could think about was Cassy riding to Sonoma State with a professor who'd been hanging around a lot lately. He struggled to make conversation. He knew Ben collected coins. He reached into his pocket. "Crossing the Golden Gate Bridge, I got a Susan B. Anthony dollar in change. At first, I thought I'd been ripped off. It looked like a quarter. Have you seen one of these?"

Ben studied the coin. "1979 P. That means it was minted in Philadelphia. At first glance, it looks like it has eleven sides, but it's round. What idiot decided to make a dollar the same size as a quarter? Some call it a Carter quarter or a Susan B. Edsel. The casinos loved them. They didn't work in vending machines, but rumor has it they worked in the quarter slot machines. I'll give you fifty cents for it." He gave the coin a closer look. "Something doesn't look right about the rim. Come inside. I'm going to get something."

In a few minutes he returned and set a metal box on the coffee table. He used a magnifying glass to look at Liam's SBS dollar, as well as one of his own that he removed from the box. "Well, I'll be. Look at this!"

All Liam saw was a slightly out of focus Susan B Anthony. "I'm afraid I don't get it."

"Your dollar is missing the rim above the words Liberty. It was improperly struck. It's flawed."

Liam clenched his teeth. So his dollar was flawed. It figured. Was anything in his life not screwed up? "I don't suppose most people would see that or even care."

"Dammit, we should care. If the government can't get little things right, you know they'll mess up the big things." Ben opened the metal box again and removed a large gold coin in a clear plastic envelope. "Ever seen one of these?"

Liam examined it. It was brilliant gold without a mark, about one-and-a-half inches in diameter and surprisingly heavy. On the front was an exquisite bas-relief sculpture of Miss Liberty holding a torch. The date was 1933. On the reverse side was an eagle. "Says it's worth twenty dollars. Is it really gold?"

Ben broke into a big smile. "It's a double eagle. They're the last gold coins ever made in the U.S. for general circulation, but they never made it. FDR weaned the country off the gold standard in '33. The Mint was supposed to melt and destroy the whole lot. Typical government waste of money."

"So...how did this one escape?"

"They say it was an inside job. Someone put his hand in the cookie jar. A bureaucrat figured it out when one was offered for sale in 1944. The Secret Service seized eight more, and they were destroyed. You'd think the Secret Service had better things to do. Hell, even King Farouk had one."

"King who?"

"Farouk, of Egypt. He had the biggest coin collection in the world."

"Well, if all the coins were melted, how did this one—"

"Hold your horses. I was about to get to that. The system broke down. Farouk had a double eagle taken out of the country because of some kind of bureaucratic mix-up."

"How'd you get this?"

"Well, I can't be sure this is the Farouk coin. There may be others. Who knows? FDR made owning gold in the U.S.

against the law, except for jewelry, but a lot of people hoarded their gold coins. My brother, Syd, was in North Africa. After one battle, he found this on a dead Nazi. This guy had all kinds of stolen loot, jewelry, and what not. Syd mailed it to me before I shipped out."

"North Africa. Was there a connection with King what's-his-name?"

"Farouk. I don't know. Could be. I'll leave this to Cassy when they take me away in a pine box."

Ben was quiet, flipping the coin between his fingers. Several times, he seemed about to say something. Finally, he said, "I wonder what this might be worth. It's got an ounce of gold in it. That alone would make it worth a few hundred. Can't be too many others out there, maybe none. I'm not sure it's even legal to have this. You're a clever guy. Could you ask around? Discreetly, of course. Hell, I don't need the money. I'm just curious."

Liam liked being called a clever guy. "I'll see what I can find out. I've got a job interview tomorrow on the Peninsula. I'll stop by a coin dealer in the city on the way."

"I'd be much obliged."

Liam picked up the double eagle the next morning and locked it in the glove compartment of his van. He arrived at the coin shop at 9:30, but found it wouldn't open until ten. He forgot to stop there on the way home, so he researched the double eagle on the Internet after dinner.

It was dark that evening when he parked in front of Ben's house. He told Storm to wait in the van and raced to the door. Cassy let him in.

"Hi." Liam kissed her on the cheek. "I've got some big news."

"You joined the marines. Just kidding. Ben told me about your job interview. Did you get it?"

"They'll let me know."

Ben burst into the room. "I've called the cops. Someone's trying to break into Liam's van. I think it's Frank."

Liam bolted for the door, but Ben caught his arm. "Wait a minute. Don't scare him off before the cops get here. I want him caught red-handed."

"But your double eagle is in my glove compartment."

"Just a minute more."

They moved to the window of a darkened bedroom. Seconds later, a patrol car pulled up, and a shadowy figure ran from the van, followed closely by Storm, who bolted through the open door.

"Halt! Stay where you are," ordered the cop. He apprehended the thief, who was indeed Frank.

Liam rushed outside, followed by Ben and Cassy. The glove compartment had been pried open, and the coin was gone. Storm seemed more curious than protective, and trotted toward Frank's truck.

Liam recognized the same cop who had arrested him. "Officer, this man just stole a valuable coin from my van. I think he wanted to frame me again."

"Is that true?" the policeman asked.

Frank fiddled with his fingers and looked away from the policeman. "No way, man."

The cop touched his holstered pistol. "Empty your pockets."

After a lot of protesting and bravado, Frank finally pulled the double eagle from his jacket pocket, as well as a baggy of yellow crystalline chunks.

The officer took the coin and handed it to Liam. "Is this the coin, sir?"

A quick look was all he needed. "Yes, that's it. A twenty-dollar gold piece. 1923. It really belongs to this man." He turned and gave the double eagle to its owner.

"Yes, this is my coin," Ben said.

The policeman motioned toward Frank's truck. "Is that your dog, sir?"

Storm's feet rested on the open window. He began sniffing and pawing the door.

"Hey! Get that dog away from my truck," Frank yelled.

Liam remembered how Storm had sniffed out Josh's marijuana at the Incredible Dog Challenge. "Officer, that truck is dirty."

Despite Frank protesting his constitutional rights, the officer checked the truck and located several kilos of marijuana and bags of crystal meth hidden behind door panels. He arrested Frank on drug charges. Ben decided not to press coin theft charges after the policeman explained he would need to keep it as evidence. Another police vehicle arrived ten minutes later, impounded the truck, and hauled it away. The officer thanked everyone and took Frank to jail.

As the police car pulled away, Ben removed the double eagle from his pocket and held it out. "Liam, has your memory gone bad? You told the cop the date was 1923. I told you yesterday it was 1933."

"Excuse my little white lie. I thought it might be best if I changed the date for the policeman's ears. You were right when you told me last night that owning this coin was illegal. There are only three others known to be in existence. Two are in the Smithsonian and one was discovered for sale last year. There may be others. If the Mint exempts the newly discovered coin, it'll be put up for auction. It could sell for millions. Maybe that one is the King Farouk double eagle. Maybe yours is. We may never know. President Ford signed a bill in 1974 making it legal to own gold again."

Ben smiled. "Well, I guess this'll be our little secret. I wouldn't sell it, anyway. It reminds me of my brother."

35 NUTS!

Sonoma County's seasonal drought ended in December with a vengeance. All day drizzles kept residents from playing golf, gardening, or working dogs on agility equipment. Other days, the skies cut loose, the downpours producing misery for all and traffic nightmares on the 101. A few miles northwest, hundreds of residents in Guerneville were stranded when the mighty Russian River once again overflowed its banks, flooding trailer parks, beachfront resort cabins, and low-lying sections of the town. A brown lake surrounded the popular waterslide park, and the dinosaur at the Peewee golf course peeked out of watery depths. There were scary moments during evacuations as large branches crashed down from the trees, and the water rose as much as one foot an hour.

One old-timer shrugged the whole thing off. "I was born here, lived all my life here, and have seen it flood a dozen times. Today is no big deal."

After the long period of gray skies, the Pacific low-pressure trough moved west to create snowy chaos in the Sierra. As the skies cleared, so did Liam's prospects. His misdemeanor conviction was overturned, and the weasel Frank was behind bars. The unexpected team trophy from the North American Championships had arrived in the mail.

His school principal, Malcolm Honeywell, called to let him know his suspension was lifted. Coming at mid-year, his old assignment teaching advanced classes was not available, but there was a full schedule of remedial classes. The principal said he'd be pleased to write an excellent recommendation if Liam accepted a transfer to another school. Liam had seen this before. When Honeywell wished to ease someone out, but had no other options, he'd make life as miserable as possible.

The following day, the private school on the Peninsula called. They knew all about Liam's brush with the law, and that it had been resolved. They offered him the track-coaching job. As an added inducement, they wanted him to accept a full teaching slate of advanced classes, replacing a teacher who was going on maternity leave.

Everything was falling into place. Later that morning, he washed the van, got a haircut, and purchased the largest diamond ring he could afford. He took a chance that evening and headed to Sebastopol. He wiped the sweat from his hands, took a deep breath, and rang the doorbell. Ben answered and explained that Cassy was having dinner with a friend.

Liam felt strangely relieved. His heart stopped racing and his vocal cords relaxed, dropping his voice from soprano back to tenor. "I should have called. I'll come back later."

Ben grabbed Liam's arm and pulled him into the house. "Sit down. I'm watching Monday Night Football. Patriots and Dolphins. How about a beer? Need a glass?"

"Bottle will be fine."

Myst jumped onto the couch. She lay down and rolled over onto her back so Liam could stroke her belly.

Ben returned from the kitchen with two bottles. "You do have a way with dogs," he said with a smile. He sat down and handed Liam a beer. "The doctor told me I've pretty much made a complete recovery."

"Great news. I'll drink to that."

The old man lifted his bottle and used it to point toward his guest. "Do you know what happened on today's date in '44?"

When they were alone together, Ben often opened up to him about the war. "Let's see, winter…December 22nd…1944…Battle of the Bulge?"

"Right. The Germans had Bastogne surrounded and ordered the Seventh Army to surrender. You know what the American General replied?"

"If I remember correctly, he said, 'Nuts!'"

"Right you are. The next day, the weather cleared and allied bombing kept the Germans at bay. A few days later, Patton arrived, and the rest is history. The news reached us in Italy and gave us hope. Maybe we'd make it home after all."

After a long pause, Liam added, "Home meant seeing Rebecca, didn't it?"

Ben's eyes misted. His voice full of gentle yearning, he said, "She was one in a thousand."

Liam didn't know quite how to broach the subject, so he just blurted out, "I feel the same way about Cassy."

Ben was quiet for what seemed like an eternity to Liam. Then he spoke. "I know. My eyes aren't what they used to be, but I'm not blind." He sat stone still for another minute before continuing. He said Cassy reminded him of his wife:

beautiful, kind, and sensitive to others. He was grateful for the happiness he had known. "No one thought she'd have me, but she did."

Liam was touched by the old man's remembrances. "I would have liked to have known her."

"Cassy will be home soon. Thanks for letting me go on so. I think I'll go to bed now. Please have another beer and make yourself comfortable." He left the room, closely followed by Myst.

Shortly before ten, Cassy arrived home. Liam showed her Storm's team trophy, and they hugged. He told her about his recent good fortune. "I've got a couple options. Accept the remedial science teaching assignment, or move on to the private school and teach honor classes. Honeywell had another choice. Transfer to another school."

Cassy listened intently. "So have you decided?"

"I've spent sixteen years at Sonoma Central High. The students…the faculty…they've been like my family. They've stood by me these last few months."

"So what are you going to tell Honeywell?"

"Nuts," he said.

"Nuts?"

"Yeah. I'm staying put. No transfer. I'm not running away."

"Well, good for you."

"Enough about me. How'd your dinner go?"

"My former sociology teacher invited me. We went to this really upscale place on the waterfront in Sausalito. I've seen him a few times this semester."

"I know I've been a pretty uncertain companion the last few months." He fumbled in his pocket and pulled out the ring box. He stammered and cleared his throat. "I've got something very important to ask you."

Before he could finish, Cassy interrupted. "He asked me to marry him."

"Whoa! Wasn't expecting that."

"Neither was I. He told me to take my time, to think about it…I've already decided"

Liam took a deep breath. "And?"

"I'll tell him tomorrow."

"Tell him what?"

She took Liam's hand. "I'll tell him…nuts." She smiled at Liam's startled look. "No, I won't use that word. I'll thank him for his interest, but I already had someone else in mind. Now, what were you going to ask me?"

The following April, the nervous bridegroom stood under a towering Sequoia in Muir Woods. Ben escorted the bride down the earthen path. Claire was maid of honor. Liam's brother, Sean, traveled from Ireland to be best man.

Cassy's mother flew down from Alaska and was an honored guest. At the reception, she and Ben had an animated discussion about San Francisco freeways that ended with a hug. The next day, Sandy took one last walk through the Haight-Ashbury. She passed on peacefully the following month.

Ben lived another two years and was buried in the Golden Gate Cemetery with other honored veterans. The newlyweds settled down in Sebastopol, where Cassy was hired to teach English. Liam returned to Sonoma Central High to teach remedial science. His students struggled on standardized tests, but won state science fair awards three years in a row. Principal Honeywell was fired the following spring for falsifying test score records in the Distinguished School application.

Myst and Storm continued their agility careers, but the story doesn't end here. There would be another shining moment in Minnesota three years later.

36 Hanging Together in Mankato

Mankato, Minnesota was the site of the greatest mass hanging in United States history, the result of a Dakota Indian uprising. Three hundred and three were condemned to die, but the list was pared to thirty-nine, and President Lincoln removed one more from the list he signed. In the end, thirty-eight Sioux were led to the gallows the day after Christmas in 1862.

It had been two weeks since the tragic events of September 11, 2001. Radio reports put the blame on a terrorist group operating out of Afghanistan. A sense of national unity and emotion gripped the country, comparable to the bombing of Pearl Harbor on December 7, 1941.

With airline travel restricted, many entrants changed their plans and drove to the finals of the North American Dog Agility Championships in the middle of September. Cassy, unable to take two weeks off from teaching, reluctantly stayed home. Liam, on sabbatical during the fall semester, made the trip. On the fourth day of his cross-country drive, he left Interstate 90 and passed through the flag-draped streets of small towns in Minnesota. That afternoon, he arrived in Mankato.

During opening ceremonies the following morning, tears welled in Liam's eyes as he listened to a remarkable voice singing "The Star Spangled Banner." He wasn't alone. The lady next to him nodded toward the soloist and whispered, "Can you believe she's still in high school?"

Next, that same pure voice sang, "Oh Canada," because many competitors came from north of the border. Only two of the qualified dog/handler teams had failed to make the difficult journey. The event was held in the Civic Center, an arena that also served as a hockey rink for the Mankato State Mavericks. The cement floor had been completely covered with watered sod and had the sharp acrid smell of the midwestern prairie after a rainstorm.

Storm was entered in the veteran's division, a category for dogs seven years of age and older. He had never placed in the top three at the Championships, although he had qualified for the finals four times. The veteran's field also included several former Grand Champions.

Because there are so few dogs in Storm's breed, the gene pool for flat-coated retrievers is not as diverse as it should be, which leads to genetic problems, particularly cancer. It's a rare flat-coat who lives beyond eight. Storm was nine. This might be his last Championship. The big goofy dog that continued to compete with the Aussies and border collies deserved a ribbon of some kind to cap off his agility career.

Border collies, bred to herd sheep, dominated the sport of dog agility. They need a job. If you don't give them work, they'll drive you nuts. Most weigh between 30-35 pounds and are able to sprint to full speed in a fraction of a second. They stop and turn faster than a UFO over New Mexico. Casual dog owners, who mistake them for ordinary dogs, may need weeks in rehab getting over the experience. Successful BC owners must have strong egos that are not threatened by dogs smarter than themselves.

Liam waited with the other handlers while officials set the course. Once the course was set, the handlers had ten minutes to walk it and plan their strategy. Waiting was the worst part, making everyone edgy. A voice from behind abruptly broke his concentration.

"You run that big black dog, don't you?"

The question came from a girl who looked to be about sixteen with magenta hair, dressed entirely in black except for the white letters on her T-shirt proclaiming, "Canadian Girls Kick Ass!" She had black fingernails and wore matching lipstick. Black eye liner highlighted her pale white makeup.

"Yes," Liam said. "I like your hair."

The girl giggled. "Yeah, I'll bet."

"I'm not shocked. I teach high school. What kind of dog do you have?"

"A couple border collies. For cripes' sake, everyone's got BC's. But I love your black dog. I mean, nobody here has a dog that big. He's like a locomotive out there. I bet he weighs more than 30 kilos."

Liam did a quick conversion in his head. Thirty kilos. About seventy pounds. She was close. He thought she looked familiar. "Weren't you at last year's event? Junior handler class. You won with the black dog, Elvira. I didn't recognize you at first."

"Yeah. I was a closet Goth last year. Skinny Jesse with braces on her teeth. God, I was so ugly."

It came back to him. Jesse Watkins. She ran like she was possessed, the most intense teenage competitor he'd ever seen. She didn't seem to fit in with the other young people, but appeared at ease with adults.

A new voice piped up. "Not only did she get first, but second as well. I'd die for any kind of ribbon."

Liam recognized the girl who had sung the national anthems.

Jesse smiled. "Well, Ingrid, this could be your year. Only a half-dozen dogs are entered in the large dog junior handler division. The other wimpy kids couldn't cut school this week. The first three get ribbons."

"What kind of dog do you have, Ingrid?" Liam asked.

"A golden retriever, but I'm afraid Rusty and I are not very good."

"No, all you can do is sing like you're ready for 'Phantom of the Opera,' get straight A's, and have a hot boyfriend with a hockey scholarship to UM."

Ingrid looked a little embarrassed. "I don't always get straight A's."

"I rest my case," Jesse said.

At 7:30 the handlers previewed the course. Because there were so many competitors, groups walked the course in shifts. The large dog veteran handlers walked the course with the juniors.

Liam pondered the teeter. A canine racing at full speed and approaching straight on might confuse this obstacle with the dog walk and go sailing into the air before the teeter tipped. The resulting "fly off" incurred a penalty of twenty faults.

After more than seven years in this sport, Liam still worried over how to get his dog safely into the yellow zones on the contact obstacles. Jesse stopped next to him.

"How are you going to handle this?" he asked her.

She clasped her hands in front of her Canadians Kick Ass T-shirt. "You know, you're pretty fast for an old guy. Why don't you just run as fast as you can and stand in his way when he runs down? That should slow him."

Liam shook his head. "I'm not sure. He'll run me over."

"You big wuss. Just stand there like a statue and don't flinch. He'll stop."

"I'll think about it."

There would be two rounds on Friday, two more on Saturday, and two concluding rounds on Sunday. The dog handler team with the fewest total faults over the six rounds would be champion. Liam preferred to be somewhat on the conservative side for the first few rounds.

He retrieved Storm from the penned area where Aussies, border collies, shelties, and a myriad other breeds howled like restless sled dogs. Many kennels had rigged little American flags to the sides. Others had Maple Leaf flags, as well as the Stars and Stripes to honor their neighbors. Storm carried a stuffed bear in his mouth to the arena, because Liam had learned that if he didn't give his dog a toy, he might try to steal one on the way, or stick his nose into someone else's treat bag. Dogs weren't allowed to take toys into the ring. No food, no collar, no toy. Those were the rules. The bear needed to be removed before entering the ring.

Storm's first run was fast and clean with no faults as he approached the dog walk. When he ascended the up plank, Liam sprinted with every ounce of speed he could muster to the front of the down plank. He wheeled around, put his hands behind his back, and froze. Storm, wide-eyed, hesitated and put all four feet in the yellow zone. They continued on, fault-free to the finish. Jesse waited outside the ring with Elvira and gave him a high five as he exited the ring.

After round one, only seven veteran dogs remained fault-free. The rankings based on faults and time had Storm in seventh place. In round two he dropped a bar, but still moved up to fifth. Jesse and her two BC's held first and second in the Junior Handler division. Ingrid and her golden were fourth.

The handlers waited while Saturday's first course was being set. Ingrid's boyfriend, Pete, was there to lend moral support. She appeared edgy and tried to make small talk. "You know, today is the first day of fall."

"Oh my God, you're so right," said Jesse. "Did you know that you can balance an egg on one end at the exact moment of the autumn solstice?"

"I didn't know that."

"Yeah. It can only happen on the first day of fall."

"Why's that?"

"Because the earth is perfectly balanced with the sun exactly over the equator."

This was too much for Pete. "You're full of crap, you ditz. First of all, the first day of fall is called the autumnal equinox. The first days of summer and winter are called solstices, and the spring equinox would have the exact same conditions as fall."

"What do you know?" Jessed shot back. "I'm talking about an egg, not a hockey puck."

"If you'd get out into the sunlight a little more often, your brain might clear up."

Ingrid jumped in. "Come on, Pete, that bites."

"Oh, crap. I'm out of here. I'll be in the stands."

Pete left, and the two girls stood silently staring into space. Jesse touched Ingrid lightly on the arm. "Thanks for sticking up for me."

"You'll have to excuse Pete. He's on edge. He's thinking of joining the Marines. You know, this 9/11 thing."

During the competition on Saturday, torrential rain, lightning, and thunder swept through Mankato. Many dogs were unnerved and had uncharacteristically flawed runs. On the other hand, the thunder and rain had no effect on Storm, who became more energized. He'd been trained as a gun dog. Despite the downpour raging outside, he had only a few time faults. Following Jesse's advice, Liam raced to beat his dog to the down plank of the dog walk and froze, but his dog had started to figure that game out. He descended faster and had only one foot in the yellow zone on his last run Saturday.

One by one, the other contenders had fallen by the wayside. The great former Canadian Champion, Ghost, a white border collie, had a fly-off on the teeter – twenty faults – and dropped from first to fourth. Storm moved into third place behind two BCs. He had a chance to get his first ribbon at the North American Championships.

Jesse had all but wrapped up first and second place in her division. Elvira was running away from the field. Her second place dog, Dark, had a big lead over third and was almost 80 points better than Ingrid's golden in fourth.

The rain relented on Sunday, but the sky remained overcast with dark threatening clouds. Liam hadn't slept well the night before. He desperately wanted Storm to win a ribbon.

The big flat-coat dropped a bar in round five, but the standings remained unchanged. While the Championships' final course was set, Liam stared off into space, lost in thought, afraid of failing. This is only a sport, he told himself. Have fun. Just do your best.

A familiar figure tapped his shoulder. "I tried the egg thing yesterday afternoon. It didn't work. I guess I am a ditz. Any last-minute advice?"

"Well, first of all, you're not a ditz. My only suggestion would be not to change. Be yourself. Don't do anything different. What advice do you have for this nervous old handler?"

"Run naked."

Jolted back to reality he replied, "Excuse me?"

"You know, don't forget to remove the collar. The dogs have to run naked. And leave the toy outside the ring."

"Good advice. Thanks. Good luck."

In the final round, the dogs ran in the reverse order of their positions. The fourth place dog, Ghost, had a spectacular run, the fastest of the day, with no faults. He had a good chance to improve his standing if another dog faltered.

Storm gave it everything he had running the last course, but looked tired. The cross-country drive and three days of competition were taking a toll on the oldest dog in the field. He lumbered to the finish with no course faults, but Liam glanced at the course clock and realized there would be time faults, one fault for each second overtime.

As Liam hurried to kennel Storm in the penning area, he heard wild cheers from the arena, as well as loud groans when Fly and Spirit had their last runs.

A figure dressed in black raced up to him, ready with a high five. Her face beamed with glee. "You did it! Fly had a ten-fault off course and dropped a bar. Spirit missed a contact."

"You mean we'll get a ribbon?"

"No, goofus. You guys were slammin'. He won the whole thing. He gets a trophy. Wish me luck. The juniors are next."

Liam, confused and muted, mouthed the words, "Good luck." He'd wait until he saw the scores posted before he believed Storm's improbable victory.

He hurried back to the arena in time to watch Ingrid and Rusty have their best effort of the weekend with only a few time faults. Jesse had a flawless run with Dark, who appeared to lock up second place. As she finished, the judge walked over to her and pointed out that Dark still had his collar on and was DQ'd. How ironic that she had cautioned him to "run naked," and then forgot herself. He felt overwhelming disappointment for Jesse, although she seemed to take it rather well. She and Elvira finished the division with a perfect run to clinch first place. After a few moments, he realized that, with Dark eliminated, Ingrid and Rusty would move into third place. Ingrid would get her ribbon. Had Jesse…?

At the victory ceremony, Liam and his dog climbed to the top rung of the award stand. Storm held the stuffed bear in his mouth. The Juniors followed. Ingrid beamed as she accepted her third place ribbon. Jesse abandoned her all black attire and wore blue jeans, a red-and-white striped shirt, and sported a new shade of blue lipstick. She smiled and waved a small American flag.

Ingrid gave her a hug. "The guys are going out for pizza. You know, just hang out. Wanna come along?"

"Well, let me check my social calendar." Jesse giggled. "Yes, I see there's a vacancy for the next five years."

37 Storm 1992 - 2003

"Just this side of Heaven is a place called The Rainbow Bridge. When an animal dies that has been especially close to someone, that pet goes to the Rainbow Bridge. There are meadows and hills for our special friends so they can run and play together. There is plenty of food and water and sunshine, and our friends are warm and comfortable. All the animals who had been ill and old are restored to health and vigor, those who were hurt or maimed are made whole and strong again, just as we remember them in our dreams of days and times gone by. The animals are happy and content, except for one small thing; they miss someone very special to them, who had to be left behind.

"They all run and play together, but the day comes when one suddenly stops and looks into the distance. The bright eyes are intent, the eager body quivers. Suddenly they begin to break away from the group, flying over the green grass, their legs carrying them faster and faster. You have been spotted, and when you and your special friend finally meet, you cling together in joyous reunion, never to be parted again. The happy kisses rain upon your face, your hands again caress the beloved head, and you look once more into the trusting eyes of your pet, so long gone from your life but never absent from your heart. Then you cross the Rainbow Bridge together..."

—*Author Unknown*

"He had heart."

That's how sports fans describe the courageous athletes who, win or lose, gave it their best shot. The old cliché, "It's not whether you win or lose, but how you play the game," applies to animals as well. The small racehorse, Seabiscuit, had heart. His match race against War Admiral in 1938 remains a classic, immortalized by a movie in 2003.

Liam could recall playing fetch with his flat-coat years ago. The ball accidentally rolled under a pyracantha bush. Storm never hesitated. He lunged into the bush and came out with a thorn in his eye. He yelped once. He blinked his eyelid several times, dislodging the thorn, before dropping the ball at his feet. With one eye closed, he begged to fetch again. Liam hurried him to the vet, who detected a scratch on the dog's cornea.

In April 2003, Storm celebrated his eleventh birthday. Distinguished white fur replaced the coal black muzzle of his youth. Although still robust, he showed signs of slowing down. When he played fetch that April, he'd lie down several yards away after a half dozen returns. After a few seconds, he was back for more. At first, Liam believed his dog was being stubborn. Gradually, he accepted the realization that the big dog was getting old.

Though Storm's times in agility had slowed somewhat, he still showed amazing energy and seemed happiest when he ran and jumped in competition. Textbooks praise the field trial skills of flat-coats. They don't develop as quickly as Labs, but once they learn their jobs they're the equal of any breed. Agility mirrored that observation. Unless Liam made a handling error, his dog qualified on any course and usually placed with the leaders.

In early June 2003 Liam traveled to Elk Grove for a trial. He was surprised to see Sara Buchanan. A month before, she had told him her mixed breed, Remington, had been diagnosed with hemangiosarcoma, a blood-fed aggressive tumor, a cancerous mass in his heart's right atrium. The cancer would eventually cause blood to leak from the heart into the pericardium.

He walked over to say hello to Sara, who was on the verge of tears. "Hi, Sara. How are you holding up?"

The tears welled up and cascaded down her cheeks. She sobbed, caught a few breaths, and tried to compose herself. "I've lost Remington."

Liam hugged Sara for a moment. No need to say anything. He understood the bond among dog owners when their companion passes away.

Storm competed sparingly that weekend. Once again, his performances were spirited, but he looked unusually tired at the end of the day.

The following Monday morning, Storm spent a few minutes outside and had breakfast. Shortly afterward, he lay down on the kitchen floor on his side, panting. He had trouble getting to his feet. Liam hurried him to the vet. An ultrasound picture showed Storm's heart was enlarged. Blood had leaked into the pericardium. Numerous white spots indicated a cancer had spread. The vet helped Storm pass to the rainbow bridge that morning.

NADAC CHAMPIONSHIPS
September 2001
Mankato, MN

Author's Note

This story is a tribute to the men, women, and dogs who pioneered American agility dog trials in the 1990's. All the dogs of those early years have passed on to the Rainbow Bridge. I hope this story honors the dogs and handlers of yesterday as well as those today.

This is a fictional account of the early days of dog agility in America. The historical fact checker should know that the varying venues have different rules that have changed in many ways over the years.

My wife, Anne, started our family's agility saga with a handsome flat-coated retriever named Tyler. She trained and competed with him for eight years. He was the first flat-coat to earn Champion trial titles in both USDAA and NADAC. His four-dog team won the NADAC Championships in 1998.

My first agility dog was a border collie rescue. We first met in November 1994. The caretaker (Foothill Dog Training) had given her a bath that morning, but Meg thought she needed a mud bath moments later. She was bug-eyed and suspicious of everything. With her pointed nose, I thought she looked like an opossum. She had to be tied to the car door when I drove her home because we didn't even have a crate at that time. When I got her home, she raced after a low flying bird – and caught it. As it turned out, that was my key to any agility success we might have later – she was movement motivated. At times during the first few months, she behaved like a wild animal and was noise sensitive. She mellowed in her golden years, became very affectionate, and no longer looked like an opossum. She won the 20" Elite Level at the NADAC Championships at Phoenix in 1997. She finished as the High in Trial Veteran in 2004 at the CPE Nationals. She earned trial Champion titles in USDAA, NADAC, ASCA, and CPE.

Anne began training and competing with a papillon named Will that we adopted in 1997. That allowed me to compete with both Tyler (1st) and Meg (2nd) in the veteran's division at the 2001 NADAC Championships.

In 2003 we added border collies Warp and Mimic to the team. Warp's mom was from Scotland, and Mimic's mom was from Ireland. The moms were rescued by Sharon Nelson and whelped in Idaho. Anne and Mimic competed in the Incredible Dog Challenge in 2010. We adopted another papillon named Apple in 2010.

The fictional adventures of Storm are loosely based on the agility career of Tyler. Myst is loosely based on a combination of adventures experienced by both Meg and Mimic. Tyler (2003), Meg (2008), and Will (2010) are waiting for us at the Rainbow Bridge.

Glossary

(As used in the novel and the sport before 2001. Dimensions may vary from venue to venue.)

AKC: American Kennel Club. For purebred or ILP'd dogs. First Agility trial in1994.

A-Frame: Two 9-foot panels 3 feet wide. 5'6" high. (Varies) Dogs must contact a 42-inch yellow zone when exiting.

Champion: The highest level of title accomplishment. Varies with venues.

Clean run: No faults in the required time or less.

Collapsed tunnel: A tunnel featuring a rigid entry barrel to which is affixed a flaring fabric chute.

Contacts/safety zones/yellow zones: Areas at the bottom of dog walk, A-frame, and Teeter-totter that the dogs are required to touch when exiting the obstacle.

CPE: Canine Performance Events. A newer venue, 2001.

Dog Walk: Usually 3 sections 12 feet long and one foot wide. Center plank 4 feet high. Up and down planks have a 42" yellow area that dogs are required to touch when exiting.

DQ: Disqualified. Wearing a collar in competition in some venues. Urinating or eliminating in the ring. Poor sportsmanship, aggression, running out of the ring, training in the ring, owner using food to motivate the dog in the ring, unsafe performance, etc.

Ex-Pen: Exercise pen. A fold-up fence of 6-8 panels. Each panel 2 feet wide and 3 feet high. Usually has a locking door. Sizes vary.

Jump Height: Varies in venues. From 4" for small veteran dogs to 24" for larger dogs. 30" at one time in USDAA.

Jumps/hurdles: 3-4 feet wide. Sometimes have side "wings" attached. Crossbars are displaceable. Jump cups allow the bars to be placed higher or lower to accommodate different size dogs.

NADAC: North American Dog Agility Council. The largest agility only venue. Formed in 1993.

Open Tunnels: 10-20 feet long. 24" diameter throughout.

PLP/ILP: Usually referred to an ILP. Purebred Alternative Listing/Indefinite Listing Privilege. Allows unregistered purebred dogs to compete in AKC events. Owner must submit a photo and description of their dog to AKC.

Q: A qualifying score. When a dog runs equal to or faster than a standard course time with the required number of faults or less. Varies with the different agility venues.

Teeter-Totter/see-saw: 12-foot plank, 12" wide. Tips on a 2-foot high fulcrum. Dogs must touch a 42" yellow zone when exiting.

Tire: A circular obstacle like a tire that the dogs jump through. 20-24" opening. The low opening is set at the same height as the hurdle/jumps for the various sized dogs.

Titling: Dogs earn title as they accumulate Q's. Novice, Open, and so on up through the higher levels.

USDAA: United States Dog Agility Association. The oldest venue. First trial in 1986.

Veterans: Typically dogs that are 7 years old or older.

Weave poles: An agility obstacle consisting of a series of 6-12 upright poles. The dog is required to enter the weave poles with the first pole on his left shoulder and weave alternately down the line.

CPSIA information can be obtained at www.ICGtesting.com
Printed in the USA
BVOW081331141112

305520BV00001B/143/P